MONSTER IN THE MIRROR

Jordan's hands stopped trembling. He poured another drink, and as he raised it to his lips, he looked into the mirror behind the bar.

Behind him stood a hooded man, clad entirely in black. His face was white and scabrous and covered in part by a skin-tight leather face mask. He wore black leather gloves and held something in his hands . . .

Jordan Manmouth screamed and dropped the tumbler; he grabbed an icepick from the bar and whirled to meet his attacker, but there was nothing behind him.

He turned toward the mirror again and the hooded figure was there, so close he thought he saw black pools of absence where the eyes should have been. In rage and fear he flung the bottle of vodka and shattered the mirror.

But in every shard, Manmouth saw a reflection of the hooded figure coming toward him . . .

VOLUME II OF
STEVEN SPIELBERG'S
AMAZING STORIES

STEVEN BAUER

C

CHARTER BOOKS, NEW YORK

STEVEN SPIELBERG'S
AMAZING STORIES
VOLUME II

A Charter Book/published by arrangement with
MCA Publishing Rights

PRINTING HISTORY
Charter edition/December 1986

ISBN: 0-441-01912-9

Charter Books are published by The Berkley Publishing Group,
200 Madison Avenue, New York, New York 10016.
PRINTED IN THE UNITED STATES OF AMERICA

CONTENTS

VOLUME II OF
STEVEN SPIELBERG'S
AMAZING STORIES

THE AMAZING FALSWORTH
by Steven Bauer

Based on the Universal Television series *Amazing Stories*
Created by Steven Spielberg
Adapted from the episode ''The Amazing Falsworth''
Teleplay by Mick Garris
Story by Steven Spielberg

FALSWORTH, THE PSYCHIC, WAS THE NEXT ACT ON, but as much as Elaine loved to watch him work, as frightened as she was to go out into the city alone these days with this serial killer loose, she had to get home. Her part in the club's lineup of acts was over for the night, and Keith was going to take her out for a late dinner. She wrapped herself tightly in her coat, whispered her good-byes to Gail who'd gotten the plum of assisting Falsworth, and slipped out through the stage door. It was winter in L.A., and it was cold. The fronds of the palms on Sunset waved in the chill wind.

The alley was dark and creepy; still slightly blind from the bright stage lights, she blinked, trying to focus. Across from her, newspapers and trash, pushed by the wind, blew up against the brick wall,

and she turned toward Sunset where streaks of
orange and blue neon flashed.

She shook her head. It was tough getting on in this
town, and this late-night stuff was wearing her out.
Another month of this, maybe, and Jimmy, the stage
manager, had promised he'd find her better work.
She pulled the coat more tightly around her and
started walking toward Sunset where the cabs
cruised.

She heard him whistling before she saw him, a big
beefy man standing in the shadows. Her breath
caught in her throat and she took a step backwards,
and laughed in fear. "You scared me!" she said.
Then she saw the wire he was winding between his big
gloved hands and her worst nightmare came true.

Barker had been out of work for months, had
taken to the streets, wandering the dark parts of town
for places to sleep. He'd spent too many nights covered by newspapers, had eaten too many meals from
dumpsters, and his instincts were slow. This alley off
Sunset was a good one though; the club where that
Falsworth did his magic act was classy and the garbage was pretty good.

He turned into the alley, holding his bottle of wine,
and saw the girl kicking, up off the ground now, held
tight against the body of the man who'd wrapped the
wire around her throat. The man pulled her deeper
into the shadows, over by the dumpster, and when
her body went limp, he threw her roughly against the
side of a car parked in the alley.

"Oh my God," Barker said, and stumbled over to
the pay phone. He slammed the door behind him,
looked over his shoulder as he jangled the receiver's
hook, and dialed 911.

When the operator came on, he said, all in a rush,
"Hurry, get the police. It's the killer, the piano wire

guy, I saw him. Just off the Strip by Olive. Damnit, hurry. No, I'm not drunk, damnit. Please, believe me. Hurry.''

Barker quickly looked over his shoulder, screamed, and dropped the receiver which fell clanking against the metal shelf. The gloved hands smashed through the side of the booth, spraying Barker with glass, and then came down over his head and jerked the blood-slick wire taut around his neck. He'd never known pain like that before as the wire sliced the rough skin. The last thing he heard was the faraway whine of police sirens coming too late.

Falsworth was glad it was Saturday night, the last show of the week. He'd be off tomorrow and Monday, and he needed the rest. His wife, Barbara, had just left him—his fourth marriage—but he couldn't blame her, as he hadn't been able to blame Natalie, Joan, or Dina. He imagined it was tough being married to a man who could tell where you'd been, who you'd seen, what you'd said and done, simply by touching you. No one but him knew how tough it was to be able to see those things.

As always, before appearing, he was jittery. The sense of power his talent gave him, the slow arc the audience always made from skepticism to awe, was both exciting and scary. The audience never knew how much power they had: If they suddenly stopped being interested in para-psychological phenomena, he'd be out of a job.

He stood near the curtain as he always did, calming, centering himself. Behind him, he could hear Gail, his assistant, talking to Jimmy who still didn't believe he was for real, even after all these weeks of packed houses. Jimmy was concerned about the merchandise, his act, and Gail was informing him in hushed tones about Barbara's departure.

"It's that power of his," Gail said.

"Come on, this's between friends," Jimmy said. "Don't give me that bull. He's a con, a very slick one, but a con like all the rest, pretty good for a colored guy. I got this cousin, he and his partner do this thing with patterns and tones of voice, very convincing. How long did it take for him to train you?"

"It's not a trick, Jimmy," Gail said. "Falsworth's for real."

Falsworth smiled; at least Gail believed, fully, in his talents. But then so had Barbara, Natalie, Joan, and Dina. The taped intro ended and Falsworth and Gail took the stage, he in his snappy tuxedo, she in her sequined bathing suit.

He knew he looked good; he was trim, and handsome, with his slim mustache, his cocoa-colored skin, his million-dollar smile. Before the audience had even finished its ovation, he closed his eyes and let Gail fasten the elaborate rhinestone-studded blindfold around his head. The darkness helped him concentrate, and the blindfold wowed the audience, even if he felt a bit foolish stumbling around in the smoke-and liquor-laced air.

"Good evening, ladies and gentlemen," Falsworth said when the audience had quieted. "Tonight I'm not going to keep you in suspense with the card tricks and pigeons up my sleeves; I'm going to get right to the heart of my act.

"I'm going to go out among you, find out who you are, if you don't mind. All I'll need to do is touch you, or some object you own, and I'll be able to tell you something about your life. I assure you this blindfold may not be seen through, so some of you young ladies may want to guide my hands." He paused for the laughter he expected and received, and then said, "Remember: It's all in the hands."

The hokey music started and he reached out for

Gail, who helped him down from the stage. By her touch, he knew she was worried, had just said good-bye to that new kid Elaine who'd left alone though the L.A.P.D. had strictly warned women not to venture out at night unescorted. The air was strangely scented, some heavy perfume he didn't know the name of, worn by someone close to the stage, and the crowd seemed a bit jumpy. But then everyone in L.A. was jumpy these days. He bumped into a chair and the audience laughed.

"Mr. Falsworth," Gail said, bringing him to a stop. "Why don't we start here?"

Falsworth reached down and groped among the empty glasses and swizzle sticks until he found two hands holding each other, a young couple. The hands separated, and he found himself touching the wrist of a pregnant woman, in her early twenties.

"Well," he said. "I'd like to congratulate this young couple on their coming blessed event. You're four months along now, aren't you? And it will be a boy, am I right?"

"How did you know?" a woman's voice said, slightly stunned.

"All in the hands, ma'am," Falsworth said. "And welcome to L.A. Always a pleasure to have honey-mooners here." He realized what he'd said, and quickly apologized, but the audience laughed and applauded. He smiled to show he'd meant no harm and let himself be dragged to another table, where he touched a shoulder wearing an old wool suit.

"A wonderful story here, ladies and gentlemen," he said, opening his arms wide. "These two brothers haven't seen one another in twenty-six years; tonight they're reunited." The audience whooped and applauded, and Gail led him on. He discovered a man who'd just been audited by the IRS, a woman whose sister had recently been diagnosed as having cancer;

neither of those was much fun for the people or the rest of the audience, and Falsworth hurried on, looking for something both surprising and pleasing.

He found himself touching a woman's thin wrist and the bracelet surrounding it. "This beautiful bracelet," he said, "is the first present you've bought yourself with the new inheritance, isn't it? Sincerest congratulations."

"But nobody knows about that," the woman said, delighted. There it was, he'd gotten his luck back. Gail led him on, and he paused and placed his hand on a man's big shoulder, and he froze.

He saw Elaine leaving the stage door; he saw the back of her head; he saw a bloody piano wire, and the corpse of a man slumped in a smashed phone booth.

Falsworth grunted in horror and stepped backwards, almost falling into the lap of a customer who'd hunched forward for a better look. He tried to say something, anything; tried to make up a pretty story to get away from this man. All he could see was that evening's headline in the *Times:* KEYBOARD KILLER STRIKES AGAIN, CLAIMS EIGHTH PIANO WIRE VICTIM.

Now the number of bodies had mounted to ten.

Elaine? He'd killed Elaine?

Falsworth stumbled sideways, not knowing what to do, pulling against Gail. He grabbed out and reached another hand, and began babbling. He could suddenly see nothing clearly; nothing was coming through. He was filled with rage and horror and terror and he knew that unless he took immediate steps, he'd feel the thin twang of a single wire around his neck.

"You're in town," he said, "for a convention. Luck with a starlet or two."

"You're wrong, mister," this man said, this man

who sat two or three tables away from the serial killer, this man who had no idea in the world of what Falsworth knew. "I'm head of the Christian Plumbers' Association in Waukegan, Illinois, and I don't have that kind of lust in my heart."

The audience laughed, but the edge was clearly gone; Falsworth was a fake after all, just as they'd suspected.

"Get me back on stage," he whispered to Gail, and she did as she was told. What should he do? What should he say? *Stop that man!* he could yell out. *Call the police!* But the vision of his own death was so strongly on him, he was paralyzed.

He stood on stage, weak, trembling. Gail stepped forward and said, "Would anyone like to send up a personal item for the Amazing Falsworth to read?"

He couldn't stand it any longer. He ripped off the blindfold and scanned the front tables, ready to point. He could hear nothing but the pounding of surf in his ears, the ocean of his own blood.

There was the young couple, the woman's ring glinting in the stage light; there was the table with the two brothers. There was an empty seat, a single.

The killer was gone.

Falsworth stumbled off stage as Gail said, "Of course these items will be returned to you . . ."

In the dark by the edge of the curtain, he ran suddenly into a man and screamed hoarsely, until he discovered it was only Jimmy.

"Falsworth, jeez," Jimmy said. "What the hell you doing? You're still on. You scared the shit outta me."

"Listen," Falsworth said. "Get the police over here. They shouldn't be far away. I'm going to my dressing room. Have them come right up. And hurry."

•   •   •

He was trembling as he turned the knob and pushed open his dressing room door. The dim light from the hallway sliced into the darkness, revealing the trunk with his magic tricks, the scarves and hoops and balls he'd used before he'd been able to convince the club owners about his other talent. He pushed the door shut, felt along the wall for the light switch, and in the dark behind him heard the exhalation of breath.

He whirled and gasped, just as he found the switch and flipped it on. The room filled with the bright lights of his makeup mirror.

A man sat in the chair before the mirror, smoking a cigarette as if he'd been waiting for Falsworth. Falsworth stood trembling, every inch of his body thrilling with fear and adrenalin, waiting for the man to make a move. He wore a coat such as the one Falsworth had touched before, but this man was slimmer than he'd imagined, and his hands in his lap held what looked like a scrap of paper instead of a piano wire.

Slowly the guy stood, and began to smile.

When the phone rang, both of them jumped.

Falsworth lunged for it and picked it up, saying, "This is Falsworth."

"Mr. Falsworth," a male voice said. "This is Detective Spota, L.A.P.D."

"Don't move," Falsworth said to the man in his dressing room. "I've got the police on the line."

"Mr. Falsworth," the voice said.

"Detective," Falsworth said. "The murderer . . . the Keyboard Killer . . . is in my dressing room, right now."

The man before him backed slightly away, an expression of bewilderment and fear on his face.

"Look, Mr. Amazing Falsworth," Spota said. "If you want publicity, call *Entertainment Tonight*. We got a job to do here."

"Look, detective," Falsworth said. "I'm a professional psychic."

"I know who you are," the cop said. "I've seen your show."

"The killer was in the club tonight, must have slipped in right after the two murders . . ."

"How do you know there were two?" the cop said.

"Because I *know*," Falsworth said. "I touched him while I was blindfolded. I could feel who he was, and what he'd just done. And now he's in my dressing room. He's right in front of me." This was insane. And he'd thought he'd been in danger before.

"Will you be all right?" Spota said.

"How the hell do I know?" Falsworth said.

"I'll be right there," Spota said, and hung up.

Falsworth picked up the phone and wielded it like a weapon, ready to bash in the guy's head with it if he tried anything funny. He was angry now, very angry, his fear having charged him with energy.

"You bastard," he said. "You killed her and you don't even care. What do you want with me?"

The guy stuck out his hand with an envelope in it, stood taller than he had before, and began to sing:

"We're better friends than we were spouses,
    Better off in separate houses;
    And though it may not seem as such,
    I love you very, very much."

"You kidding me?" Falsworth said. "A singing telegram? You pulling my goddamn leg?"

"It's from your loving ex-wife Natalie," the guy said. "Can I go now?"

Falsworth fumbled with the envelope he'd been handed; Western Union, all right, with the silly message printed out in teletype letters. "Jesus," he said. "Yeah, get the hell out of here. Thanks for the cheap thrills."

"I almost forgot," the guy said, reaching into his jacket and pulling out a big chocolate chip cookie on a stem. Then he brushed past Falsworth and out the door, slamming it behind him.

Falsworth was exhausted; all the adrenaline had left him, it seemed. In the stranger's wake, the dressing room had the creepy silence of the middle of the night. He locked his dressing room door, poured himself a stiff bourbon, and sank into the chair before his makeup mirror. So much for the famous million-dollar smile. He looked like hell.

But the adrenalin began to return with every minute he was alone. He ate the cookie, finished the bourbon which seemed, tonight, to have no effect. He drummed his fingers on the chair's arms, but even that didn't do much to interrupt the horrible silence. He got up, paced, and then stopped, his heart pounding in his ears. Outside, in the hall, someone was approaching.

The footsteps stopped before his door. In the light filtering through the crack he saw the shadow of a pair of men's shoes.

He almost stopped breathing; the feet didn't move. He searched the room quickly, looking for something he could use as a weapon, cursing himself for not having looked earlier—a letter opener, an ashtray. Was there anything in his trunk? He tried to think.

The silence was broken by a loud ham-fisted pounding.

"Who is it?" Falsworth asked, ashamed at how shaky his voice sounded.

"Detective Spota, L.A.P.D.," a voice said, the same voice he'd heard over the phone.

In a rush, Falsworth walked to the door and threw it open. Spota was wearing a beige trench coat, blue slacks, horn-rimmed glasses—a big, bearish, friendly-looking man. "Mr. Falsworth?" he said. "You okay?"

"Thank you for coming, detective," Falsworth said. "You scared the hell out of me."

"Where's the suspect?" Spota said.

Falsworth blushed. "I'm sorry, detective," he said. "It was, uh, a case of mistaken identity."

"You telling me the killer's not here?"

"He is, I swear it. It just wasn't who I thought it was."

"Look," Spota said. "I want you to know, right off the bat, that I don't believe in that psycho-phenom . . . whatever the hell you call that crap you do."

"Para-psychological phenomena," Falsworth said.

"Whatever," Spota said. "Me and Joe Friday, all we're interested in are the facts. Now you may have made a nice little career out of mind reading, and I respect that, I really do. But I've made a career out of fact finding for the past nineteen years, and I hope you'll respect that. Now what the hell happened here?"

Falsworth let Spota in; he could see the guy was going to be hard to convince. Maybe if he proved it . . . maybe if he just touched Spota's hand, told him something about himself that Falsworth couldn't possibly have known . . .

"Detective, let me . . ."

"Just tell me what happened," Spota said. "Just give me the facts."

"In my show," Falsworth began, sinking into the chair, "I wear a heavy blindfold, and my assistant leads me through the audience. When I touch them, I can see things about them, I can kind of sense details about their lives. But when Gail led me up to one man and I touched him, I felt he'd just killed two people." He paused to take a deep breath. "It was the serial killer, the guy in the papers."

"What did he look like?"

"I don't know. I was wearing a blindfold. By the time I got the courage to take it off, the guy was gone. I never saw his face."

Spota snorted and shook his head, as though he was used to dealing with loonies. It made Falsworth angry. "I didn't see his face, all right? I don't get to choose what I see."

"Listen, Falsworth," Spota said. "I'm a cop. I got to ask these questions. Could you tell me where he lives?"

"Maybe if I'd had contact for a few more seconds. I just let go of him right away. It was quite a shock."

"I'm sure," Spota said, looking around the room. "Well, I don't know where to go from here. You don't know what the guy looks like, don't know where to find him. You see, Falsworth? All day long I get calls from people like you." He turned to go.

"No," Falsworth said. "You can't leave. Don't you see? He knows who I am. He knows that I know. I'm next. Why would I make something like this up? I need your protection. I'm a dead man unless you help me."

"I'm sorry," Spota said. "I can't provide protection for everyone in the city who's scared out of his wits by this guy. Unless you got something else for me, I got to go."

In a panic, Falsworth tried to stall. Then he had an idea. "Maybe if I touched the chair he sat on, who knows? It depends how long he was there, if anyone else sat down after. I don't know. Come on, what do you say? It's worth a try."

He stood on the stage, Spota next to him. The room was filled with tables and chairs, dark, creepy, not at all the way it looked when filled with half-drunk patrons out for a good time. He walked down from the stage, as Gail would have led him. Which table? Where had the guy sat?

He got down on his hands and knees and crawled, placing both hands on the seat cushions, shaking his head as he went. The pregnant woman, her husband, the brothers . . .

He found a chair and started laughing.

"What?" Spota said.

"This guy just laid his boss's wife," Falsworth said. Spota wasn't amused. He moved to the next chair and laughed again; the woman who'd sat there —well, she had some ideas about what she wanted to do if she ever got him alone.

When he found the chair he'd been looking for, he was as shocked as he'd been before, but this time he didn't let go. He was in the alley; it was cold, and the trash and newspapers blowing around crackled in the silence. He heard some whistling, a tune he thought he knew. It was an opera, something by Verdi. He started to sweat; his knees were weak. His fingers began to tremble. Gloves, a quick twist of piano wire, Elaine's lovely neck, shattered glass, blood.

He closed his eyes and tried to breathe evenly. "There's a house," he said. "No. An apartment. On the top floor; there's a piano. It's very sparsely furnished. There are numbers, an address. It's in East L.A. By the San Bernardino Freeway. 36488 Marengo Street."

"Let's check it out," Spota said.

They left by the stage door. "He came in this way," Falsworth said as he pushed against the heavy metal. "I can feel him." Outside, the cops, the corpses were gone. Falsworth saw the smashed phone booth, blood on the glass. There was nothing out there but the trash and the wind.

Spota had had him stay in the car while he checked

the mailbox, rang the bell, got the phone number from the super, called. No one had answered. "He's not in," Spota said. "Want to come up with me?"

"What's his name?" Falsworth said.

"Scott," Spota said. "Bill Scott."

"That's not his real name," Falsworth said. "It doesn't feel right."

"Maybe this is the wrong place, then."

"No," Falsworth said. "I don't think so."

"You coming?" Spota said.

"I'm not sure I want to go up there."

"Gimme a break, " Spota said. "You're the guy's got me running around on this wild goose chase. Come on."

Falsworth thought about it a second and realized he'd rather be with the cop than sitting alone in the dark and cold. They walked quietly up the steps to the top floor, to Apartment 6-C. When they finally reached the door, Spota knocked, then pulled out a credit card and easily slipped the lock.

"Don't you need a warrant?" Falsworth asked, and Spota looked at him as though he were crazy.

The minute they entered, Falsworth knew he'd been right; he couldn't quite tell why, but the place looked as he'd seen it before, and the vibes it gave off were the ones he'd felt earlier that evening. It was very much a bachelor's quarters, sparsely furnished, no sense of design. The walls were white, and hung with framed posters from opera premieres. A sophisticated stereo system sat on a walnut table. In another corner was a color TV and a VCR. The piano, a baby grand, stood in the room's center; on one of the walls, a mounted elk's head. The guy was a hunter, a real killer. Falsworth shuddered; he was cold clear through.

He peeked in the kitchen which held a clutter of dirty dishes and hastily eaten food. One plate held a small heap of what looked like chicken bones. He began to lose his fear, began to give in to his talent. "The guy's quite a pig," he said to Spota as he came out of the kitchen. Spota stood in the middle of the room, calm, as though wondering what to do next.

Falsworth began touching things, a jacket which lay on the couch, letters on a desk. Images began coming to him: The guy had gone to college, UCLA, had majored in music history. He'd been married, was no longer. He was about six feet tall, brown hair, a big fleshy face, big hands.

He played the piano. He played well.

Falsworth looked up; Spota was watching him, fascinated.

"What do you see?" Spota said.

"The guy lives for music, now. He was very much in love with his wife, but they're obviously no longer together."

"That so?" Spota said.

Falsworth walked to the piano and began idly pressing keys. He started at the bottom of the keyboard and monotonously worked his way up. C, C sharp, D, D sharp, E, F . . . The F didn't sound, just a dull thud as the hammer hit nothing. Falsworth played it again.

"Jesus," he said. "I think I know what he's been doing."

"And what's that?" Spota said, moving closer. "Come on, reach out and touch someone, Mr. Falsworth. It's all in the hands, everything you ever wanted to know about Charlie Spota." He grabbed Falsworth's hand before it could hit another note, and the realization of how he'd been duped went through Falsworth like an electric shock.

Spota let go and casually walked to the door, bolting it. "I'm impressed, Falsworth," Spota said. "You're pretty good. Dumb, but pretty good." Falsworth could hardly breathe. He watched this man who'd killed ten people, this man who'd passed himself off as a cop and made Falsworth believe it—he'd been a fool, had never asked to see the man's badge, he'd been so frightened; Spota had never suggested, as a cop would have, that they step out into the alley, to the scene of the crime—he watched him, and loathed him, and was terrified.

"I've never done this so close to home before," Spota said. "Real convenient. You may spoil me."

"Please," Falsworth said. He could hardly speak. "I won't tell anyone."

"That's right," Spota said. "You won't." Falsworth watched as Spota took some wire cutters from his pocket, walked to the piano, and snipped a piano string loose. "Look what I've got for you," he said. "An F sharp. What do you think of that?"

"I swear to God," Falsworth said. "And who would believe me? I'm a psychic, for God's sake. A mystic, someone you read about in the tabloids. Nobody believes that stuff."

"I do," Charlie Spota said. "You've made a believer out of me." He took a pair of gloves from his coat pocket, slipped off his coat and glasses and dropped them on a chair.

"Jimmy never called the police, did he?" Falsworth said. He watched in horror as Spota smiled and shook his head.

"What . . . what did you do to Jimmy?"

"You're the psychic, Mr. Amazing Falsworth. You tell me; read what I've done with him." He reached out and beckoned to Falsworth, palms up, as if about to offer him a gift. "I never expected to enjoy this," he said. "Not like the women."

Spota slipped the gloves on, and began twisting the ends of the F sharp string around his hands. Very slowly, he began approaching Falsworth.

"It's the music, isn't it?" Falsworth said. "A different note, a different string for each of your victims."

"Except the bum tonight who surprised me," Spota said. "He got the same note as the girl."

"And you'll stop killing when all the notes play a certain song, am I right? What's the song, Spota?"

Falsworth began edging away, trying to keep the same distance between them, looking around for something he could use to protect himself, someplace to go. He moved toward the bedroom door. Spota just kept coming, slowly, wordlessly, smiling.

"It's an opera, right?" Falsworth said. "Something by Verdi."

"You're very clever," Spota said. "Very clever indeed. I wouldn't have thought a man like you would know anything about opera." He smiled. "But you're right. It's Verdi. From *A Masked Ball*. 'Eri Tu.' Unfortunately, it's a very long aria." He was breathing heavily now, and his fleshy face was very red. "It's all about a wife's betrayal of her husband with his best friend."

He lunged for Falsworth, who moved backwards in his terror against the bedroom door, which opened. He lost his balance and fell, and Spota, who'd thought to catch him, was caught off guard and stumbled over him. Falsworth looked around wildly, took in the immense space of the bedroom in which a single bed stood alone. The walls were hung with game birds. Falsworth scrambled to his feet, and Spota, having him cornered now, walked swiftly to a tape deck and flipped the ON switch. Above the passionate strains of "Eri Tu" playing at full volume, Spota yelled, "Go ahead, Falsworth. Make all the noise you want."

Spota stood, slightly out of breath, and to Falsworth his madness seemed to swell along with the music. Falsworth backed into a closet door, and knew immediately that Spota's hunting rifle was within. He whirled, flung open the closet, threw himself inside, and pulled the door shut behind him.

It was dark in the closet and Falsworth was panting as he tried to hold the door shut with one hand while he searched for the rifle with the other. He had no time; already Spota was on the other side yanking furiously. Falsworth was crazy with fear; with each of Spota's lunges, the door opened a little and light flashed in. Outside, in the full grip of his mania, Spota began singing along with the tape.

Then he found it on the floor, in its leather case. Even if he were to get it out, would it be loaded? Could he hope for that?

Spota gave the door an especially vicious tug, and Falsworth heard wood splinter as the door came loose of its hinges and Spota staggered backwards under the weight of the door he'd ripped down. His chest heaving, Falsworth pulled at the rifle and had it half out when Spota, now singing in a demented, hysterical falsetto, threw the door aside and flew at him, whipping the piano wire around Falsworth's neck; in his haste and fury, he caught the gun barrel as well. The wire twisted, cutting into Falsworth's neck.

In one quick action, struggling wildly, Falsworth managed to slip the gun barrel out from under the wire and replace it with his hand. Spota tightened his grip instantly, and as the wire cut into his throat and fingers, Falsworth cried out in pain, a strangled cry, and dropped the rifle.

Spota's singing was insane, the music deafening. Even as he was choking to death, even as he felt the blood running down onto his wrist, Falsworth groped on the floor for the rifle. Spota's strength seemed monumental. He was taller than Falsworth and the psychic felt himself being lifted further and further from the gun.

Then the balance shifted, and they both fell; in that moment, Falsworth caught and held the rifle, pulled it with him as Spota again positioned himself behind and began pulling upwards with all his strength. Falsworth tilted the gun, trying to push its stock against the floor as he groped for the trigger with his few free fingers, but now the barrel swung until it was right between the psychic's eyes.

He was losing consciousness; he was gone. His finger found the trigger and his head flopped forward and the downward motion of both shifted things just slightly, just enough so that Falsworth felt the cold nuzzle of steel on his cheek, and the blinding flash of heat as the gun discharged. The stranglehold on his neck ceased, and he fell to his knees gasping for breath.

The gun's explosion still reverberated among the passionate strains of Verdi. Falsworth drew in a long, racking, ragged breath and turned to see Spota on his back, half of his head blown away.

He retched but nothing came up. He dragged himself to the phone and punched 911. When the operator came on the line, he said, barely able to talk, "The police. Get me the police."

"Your name, sir?" a polite female voice said in his ear, another voice, a human voice, not the voice of a demented killer.

"Falsworth," he said. "That's right. The Amazing Falsworth. No, I can't read you over the phone. It's all in the hands."

Then the connection was made. A voice said, "L.A.P.D., emergency line." Falsworth was suddenly too drained to speak. "Hello? Hello?" the voice said. "Is anyone there?"

With the strains of *Un Ballo in Maschera* soaring in the background, the Amazing Falsworth gave the address.

MIRROR, MIRROR
by Steven Bauer

Based on the Universal Television series *Amazing Stories*
Created by Steven Spielberg
Adapted from the episode "Mirror, Mirror"
Teleplay by Joseph Minion
Story by Steven Spielberg

JORDAN MANMOUTH SAT WATCHING THE YOUNG couple kissing on one of the newer graves, before an immaculate tombstone; behind them a gentle breeze began stirring the bare branches of one of the maples. They were in their teens, as he'd imagined them, and the boy had just begun unbuttoning the girl's blouse when the skeletal hand reached up out of the earth and grabbed the girl's ankle.

She screamed, of course, before she even knew what had grabbed her, but when she looked down and saw the bones wrapping her leg, the arm connected to those fingers, the whole rotting corpse rising from the ground, she screamed even harder. Its face was the unearthly white of a full moon in Los Angeles, and as wrinkled as a dessicated apple; shreds of skin fluttered from its cheeks. On its head was a cap of black matted hair, and rotting teeth

25

hung in its putrid face as it opened its mouth to eat.

The boy wrenched the girl to her feet and pulled her out of the zombie's grip; he was bellowing now like a steer being led to slaughter. The two of them, shaking and trembling, bolted for the graveyard's gate, but the earth beneath them began to shift. It split open before them and from the rent graves three more bodies rose, with outstretched arms and open mouths . . .

Very nice effects, very nice indeed, Manmouth thought as the houselights came back on; the audience giggled and groaned and applauded as Dick Cavett smirked to show how silly he thought the whole horror book/movie phenomenon was. God! Manmouth thought, how he hated these wretched publicity tours, how he hated, in fact, every one of those fans out there who'd made him the world's best selling horror novelist. Why did people have to have faces and hands that wanted to touch you, and questions and . . .

"We're here with Jordan Manmouth," Dick Cavett intoned. "The author of *Screamdreams*, as well as, among others, *Decomposing Bodies* and *Attack of the Grislies*. Now that was an interesting clip, Jordan. Some members of our audience seemed offended by that scene while others thought it was funny. And you're smiling, as if you enjoyed their reaction."

"I *did* enjoy it, Dick," Manmouth said. "Movies like that *should* make the audience react. If they just sat there, I'd be worried."

"So it doesn't matter when people don't like your movie . . ."

"I wrote the book, Dick," Manmouth reminded him, "not the movie. But I don't write to be *liked*, if that's what you mean. I write because I . . . I don't know why I write."

"To make money?" Cavett asked, and the audience laughed.

"That too," Manmouth conceded.

"So tell me your candid reaction to the film. Did it do your book justice? I mean, you're the *real* star of the picture; your name is what will bring people to the theater."

"I like things in it, Dick," Jordan explained. If he could just get through this last interview, the publicity tour would be over; how many times could he answer the same question? "I like the zombies we just saw. There's a chainsaw killing that's very effective, and another scene in which a hooded strangler creeps up behind the girl. That's terrifying, I think."

Then Cavett asked the question Manmouth couldn't answer. "Where do all these horrors come from? These mutilations, grotesqueries. You think them up, of course, and they've made you rich. But do you have nightmares? Are these phantasms and demons somehow a mirror of you, the man?"

"Do I look like a ghoul?" Jordan Manmouth said and smiled. The audience hooted and whistled, loving it. For Manmouth, at thirty-nine, could have been a matinee idol. He was tall, slim, impeccably groomed and expensively dressed; he was charming, seductive, adroit in conversation. He was recently divorced, a big news item in the *Enquirer* and the *Star*. And he knew he figured quite prominently in the dreams of his female fans. With his close-up on the back of the jacket of every book, he knew he scared them with the text, then soothed them to sleep with his picture. But where *did* those horrors come from?

A studio limousine was waiting at curbside, and he jumped in the back, slammed the door quickly, and sank back in the rich upholstery. The driver immediately stepped on the gas; it was over—Jordan Manmouth was going home.

They drove several miles through downtown traffic in perfect silence, but as the chauffeur entered the winding residential area where Manmouth lived, he cleared his throat and said, "A very good show, Mr. Manmouth."

"Thanks very much," Jordan said, and hoped he could leave it at that.

"Don't those creepy stories give you the willies?" the driver asked. "They sure give me the heebie jeebies."

"I don't get scared by that stuff," Manmouth said. "But as long as other people do, I'll keep churning it out. You don't really believe in vampires, zombies, monsters—you just like to be frightened. It's the real stuff that frightens me; talk show hosts, press agents, ex-wives, alimony payments, people who ask questions."

That shut him up. The driver didn't say another word until he drew up under the portico of Manmouth's expensive house. "Here we are, sir," the driver said. Manmouth could tell he'd lost a fan.

"Thanks," he said. "God, do I hate publicity tours."

He handed the driver a twenty to ease his conscience, grabbed his small bag, and hurried up the long series of slanted granite steps to the front door. A body was huddled on the welcome mat, and Manmouth grunted in surprise. The noise woke the body; it was a kid, disheveled and pimply, a gawky, ugly kid who stood up nervously clutching a book and a manila envelope.

"What the hell are you doing on my doorstep?" Manmouth yelled. His heart was pounding; the kid had startled him.

The kid began stuttering in an agony of embarrassment. "I . . . I . . . I'm sorry Mr. Manmouth, but could you, uh like, would you . . ." He thrust a copy of Manmouth's latest novel, *Screamdreams*, at him. "Sign my book?"

"No, I won't sign your book. You're trespassing on my property. This is my home. Get out of here."

"But I'm, like, I'm your biggest fan in the world. I've got all your books, every edition, hardcover and paperback. And . . ." He shoved the book toward Manmouth and the envelope spilled from the crook of his arm, pages littering the ground at his feet.

"And you're a writer and you'd like me to read your stuff, right? I don't do business at home, kid." He looked with distaste at the trembling figure, the papers scrawled with cursive. "But here's a little advice. Learn to type." He opened the door with his key and slammed it behind him. The noise echoed in the amplitude of his pristine living room.

He grabbed the mail which lay in a pile at his feet, slung his bag over his shoulder, and started up the curved stairs to the second floor. As he walked, he sorted, letting the advertising circulars, the bills, the fan mail fall at his feet. Greta, his housekeeper, had done her job well, as usual. The carpet still held the vacuum cleaner's strokes. Fresh roses gleamed in a vase on the glass coffee table below him, and the calm pink walls radiated peace and warmth.

In the bedroom Manmouth undressed hurriedly, flung open the louvered doors, and entered the bathroom, a huge space with mirrors on half the walls and an oval sunken marble tub. He turned the faucets on full, squeezed some bath gel into the rushing water, and as steam drifted lazily upwards, he confronted himself in the mirror. His eyes were bloodshot, and his skin looked slack. He stretched his cheeks until they were taut again. "You look pooped," he said. Then he pivoted, admiring the taut muscles of his abdomen, and slapped his stomach with his palm. "Pretty good for a writer," he said, and winked at himself.

The water was hot, as he liked it, and he sunk beneath the surface bubbles until only his head rested on the rim of the marble tub. With his toes he reached up and shut off the pounding water. In the gleaming chrome, he thought he caught a flash of movement and he whipped his head around, but there was nothing there. Calm down, Jordan, he thought as he allowed himself to sink completely underwater, blowing bubbles, letting the warmth of the water drain the tension from his body.

He soaked a few minutes, then stood; he wrapped himself in a huge terrycloth towel and went to the sink under the mirror, now completely clouded with steam, to brush his teeth. With his hand, he wiped a swath of moisture away and in the small mirrored space saw his own face. And behind him, across the room, another face—grim, white, barely discernible.

Jordan gasped and spun around. He was alone in his room. Across from him the double French windows looked out over his estate. He grinned, amazed at how tired he was, so tired he was seeing things, and turned back to the mirror.

He opened his mouth to brush his teeth and saw the face again. It was a little like the face of the zombie in the movie clip, dissolving even as he watched. Its tall black body was visible now as it began climbing through the window.

Manmouth yelled and turned around, his heart pounding in his throat. He was suddenly very angry. That goddamn kid, he thought. If it was him, he'd have the police here so fast . . . He strode to the windows, flung them open, and screamed, "Get out of here, you creep. If I catch sight of you again, the police . . ."

But there was no one in the garden below. In the

clear night sky, the white moon hung huge and oblivious to human terror. He shut the windows with a bang, pulled the drapes, and stalked across the room toward the bedroom beyond. As he went, he couldn't keep his eyes from searching the mirror, and in it he saw the figure moving toward him.

He dropped the towel and ran naked and yelling into the bedroom, slamming the louvered doors behind him, snapping the latch. He put on his terrycloth robe and sat on the edge of the wide bed, shivering. What was going on? He'd never had waking dreams before. Sure, he'd had nightmares—everyone had them. But never like this, never when he was awake. He stared at the louvered doors, as though he expected a solemn knocking.

But the night was totally quiet; he strained to hear the noise of a car, a barking dog, anything. All he heard was the blood pounding in his temples. Was he going crazy? Could he be that tired?

He reached for the phone on the nightstand and quickly punched the seven digits of Karen's number. They'd just begun seeing each other, and she wasn't committed to him, but if she were home, he'd ask her . . .

"Hello," Karen's sultry voice said.

"Karen, it's me," Manmouth said. "Jordan. Can you come over? I need—"

"This is Karen," her voice said. "I can't come to the phone right now, but please, *please* don't hang up. Leave a message and let me know I didn't waste two hundred dollars on this machine. Thank you." The machine beeped, and the tape began rolling.

"It's Jordan," Manmouth said. "I've missed you. Please call as soon as you can." He hung up, and sat there breathing hard, hoping he hadn't sounded too hysterical. Women, he'd learned, didn't like hysterical men.

He had to get a grip; there was nothing wrong. He

stood, took a deep breath, and walked to the louvered doors, unlatched them and looked inside. The bath was still full, the bubbles slowly disappearing. The room was empty, totally empty except for the towel he'd discarded as he fled to the bedroom. He closed the doors again and latched them, and hurried downstairs to his den where he kept the liquor.

It was a spacious, well-lighted room, and Manmouth hit every switch. His IBM PC was centered on a large mahogany table; two of the walls were lined with bookshelves, one entire shelf holding the collected works of Jordan Manmouth. The other walls held framed posters—*Wives for Dinner*, *Haitian Zombie Honeymoon*—of the movies made from his books. He sat down in his leather chair and tried to keep his knees from shaking.

But it was no use. He stood, took a deep breath, and walked to the bar, where he poured himself a tumbler of Stolichnaya and drank it down straight. Almost immediately his hands stopped trembling. He poured another drink, and as he raised it to his lips, he looked into the mirror behind the bar.

Behind him stood a hooded man, clad entirely in black. His face was white and scabrous and covered in part by a skin-tight leather face mask. He wore black leather gloves and held something in his hands . . .

Jordan Manmouth screamed and dropped the tumbler; he grabbed an icepick from the bar and whirled to meet his attacker, but there was nothing behind him, just the den in which he'd written his books, the solid expensive furniture, the rich wine-colored carpet.

He turned toward the mirror again and the hooded figure was there, so close he thought he saw black pools of absence where the eyes should have been. In rage and fear he grabbed the Stolichnaya and flung it at the mirror. The bottle burst, spraying vodka everywhere. And the mirror shattered.

But in every shard, Manmouth saw a reflection of the hooded figure coming toward him, dozens of them raising their hands at him. He whirled around to find nothing behind him. "Give me a fucking break!" he screamed and stalked out of the den, slamming the door behind him.

He bolted every door in the house, shut and locked every window, pulled every drape. He tried Karen again, but her tape-recorded voice was no help. He huddled at the top of the stairs with nothing before or behind him but carpeting; a loaded pistol lay on the step beside him. He held the hall phone on his lap and punched the seven digits of the L.A.P.D. "You have reached the Police Department," the computerized voice informed him. "All of our lines are busy now, but please hold. All calls are being answered in order." Manmouth looked at the clock on the wall. It was 12:01. He was still holding at 3:27 when he fell into exhausted sleep.

He awoke at 9:03 to the monotonous beep of a phone left off the hook, feeling foolish, wretched, still exhausted. He showered, shaved, dressed, opened every room in the house looking for some reason for his foolishness the night before. How could he have been so frightened? How could he have imagined a figure stalking him? Manmouth tried to remember if he'd ever been so terrified, and remembered a recurring dream he'd had as a child, a dream in which his parents stood by stolidly as he screamed for help, as a . . .

He wiped the memory from his mind. He thought of his fans with more disdain than ever; why would someone enjoy being frightened? Why would someone pay good money . . .

The den was a shambles, but as he pulled the drapes and sunlight flooded the room, he was relieved to find there was nothing there but what he, Jordan Manmouth, had bought and placed there. He stayed away from the bar. Greta would clean it up.

Outside it was brilliant and clear. The smog was totally gone, and the sky was a deep cerulean. Azaleas, hydrangeas, rhododendron were in bloom and their sweet smells drifted through the air as he drove toward Century City for a meeting with the executive producer of *Screamdreams*.

He drove his car up to the gatehouse, where he stopped in line to get his ticket. He was a little late, impatient, and ready to get on with the business of being a millionaire, a hot property, an adult. The guy in front of him was asking the guard about something and Jordan hit the horn once. Behind him he heard the sound of another car rolling to a stop, and the driver of that car, also impatient, leaned on his horn.

Manmouth stole a glance in his rearview mirror, curious. Maybe he knew the driver. But all he saw was the leather-clad face of his attacker coming at him from the back seat. In his black-gloved hands, he held a strangler's cord.

Jordan screamed, flung open the door, and bolted from the driver's seat. The security guard looked up from talking, and another guard standing idly by moved toward him. On his hip was a holster.

Jordan ran to the man and grabbed his arms.

"Sir," the man said. "Your car . . ."

"He's trying to kill me," Jordan yelled. "He wanted to strangle me." He shook the man, trying to get him to understand.

"What?" the man said. "Sir, your car."

Jordan released the man and turned around. He didn't know the driver of the car behind his, but now the man was shaking a fist at him. "You have to move your car," the guard said. "You can't leave it sitting there."

Jordan took a deep breath and turned back toward the man. "I'm telling you someone is trying to kill me."

In the guard's mirrored glasses he saw the hooded figure raise the cord. Jordan screamed and hit the man as hard as he could. The guard staggered backwards; his glasses flew from his face and fell to the asphalt. With the heel of his shoe, Jordan Manmouth ground the glasses to powder as the guard drew his gun and told him to put his hands up.

He had never been in jail before, and he found the experience less than pleasant. In the holding tank he kept as far away as possible from the winos, pimps, and pickpockets with whom he shared the space. In his Pierre Cardin suit, a little rumpled and dirty, he hunched in a corner by the iron bars, waiting for Karen. When the big guy came up and said, "Gimme some money, slick," he broke.

He turned, as though this man were the one who wanted to kill him, and kicked the guy in the abdomen. "Get the hell away from me!" he screamed. He could see from the faces of the others that they thought he was crazy. Who cared? "You guys give me any more crap and I'll rip your hearts out with my bare hands," he said. They left him alone.

He felt more and more as if he was spiraling into a nightmare. Wait till the tabloids got a hold of this. MONSTER MAVEN ARRESTED FOR FREAKY DREAMS; MURDER EVERYWHERE, SAYS JORDAN MANMOUTH.

He was grunting like a cornered animal when the attendant finally came with Karen. For some reason, she thought the whole thing was funny. "I can't take you *any*where," she said.

"Just get me *out* of here," he said, and let her take his hand and drag him out of jail.

They were zipping along Mulholland Drive in Karen's Karmann Ghia, and he was ashamed and embarrassed, but nothing she said could dissuade him of what he'd experienced.

"Let me get this straight," she said for the tenth time. "Somebody's trying to kill you, but you only see him in the mirror. You turn around and he's gone." Jordan nodded tensely. "Honestly, Jordan," she said. "I like the scene in *Blood Market* better; you know, when the girl sees the rotten corpse of her uncle every time she makes love to her husband."

"Goddamn it, Karen," he said. "I'm not talking plot here. This is for real." From her face, he could see she didn't believe him, but did believe he was in trouble—a breakdown, obviously, too much work, too much exposure.

"Home or office," she said as blithely as she could manage.

"Home, I guess," he said. Even he could hear how broken his voice sounded.

Greta was cleaning up shards of glass when they entered the den, and she looked up at Jordan with undisguised disgust.

Karen pointed to where the mirror had been. "That one?"

Jordan wouldn't go near it. "Among others," he said.

He watched as she went up and stared into the hanging shards. "There's nothing here, Jordan," she said. "Just me. Over and over and over."

He let her take him upstairs to the bathroom, where it all had begun. "Come on," she said as gently as possible, as though she were dragging a recalcitrant child to the scene of a silly fright. He refused to look in the mirror. He studied the tub full of cold scummy water, the French windows through which his attacker had first approached, the stacks of clean and folded towels. "Jordan," Karen said. "Come on." Then she put her hands on her hips and made her voice as low as she could, mimicking him. "Oh, I never get scared," she said. "I just wish I could get scared. Nothing ever scares me."

"Don't make fun of me," he said. He walked up at an angle; he could see her wide brown eyes, her hair, her calm serious expression. He allowed himself to get closer, to look at himself. Behind him, in black, inches away, the figure raised the garotte over Jordan Manmouth's head. He screamed and spun around; he turned back to the mirror and the figure was closer than ever. "That's him," Jordan screamed, pointing a finger. Then he hit the floor.

"Jordan, there's nothing there," Karen said.

"In the mirror, in the goddamn mirror," he said.

She was terrified now; his terror had infected her and she was screaming. "There is nobody— *nobody*—in the goddamn mirror, Jordan. Nobody but me."

He kept his eyes tightly shut and groped his way across the floor toward where the louvered doors were, toward the bedroom which, thank God, had not a single mirror.

He lay face down on the bed, shaking, clutching a pillow. He could feel Karen's hand stroking his back as if he were a cat. "Are you okay?" she said. "I'm right here with you."

"Do I seem okay?" he said into the pillow. "Is this how I usually am?" He started sobbing, found himself unable to stop. She let him cry, kept stroking him, until the clenching in his belly subsided. He turned on his back and stared at her through blurry eyes. "I'm going nuts, Karen."

She shook her head in pity and wonder. "Is there anything I can do?" she said.

He gave her instructions. She drew every curtain in the house in case he saw himself reflected in the glass. She covered every mirror with a bedsheet. On every shiny tile floor, she lay down newspapers as though they were training a dog. In the kitchen and the bath, she took a can of black spraypaint and coated the chrome with flat dull paint. She turned every picture under glass to the wall, rolled the TV into a closet. She took his Vuarnet sunglasses and put them in the trash.

He sat in the living room huddled under blankets, but he couldn't stop shivering. He'd refused a drink, a sandwich, chicken broth, ice cream. The room was a disaster. The glass coffee table was covered with newspapers; the vase with the roses was gone—too shiny. He could see that Karen's patience was running thin, that soon she would suggest they call a doctor. When she did, he would tell her to go ahead.

"You want some coffee?" she asked. He had to get back on his feet somehow; he had to get something into his stomach.

"Okay," he said.

"I'll get it," Karen said, and began walking toward the kitchen. He was terrified of being alone, had to stop himself from calling her name. He was about to squelch what little pride he had left and tell her to forget the coffee when the doorbell rang.

Manmouth was paralyzed. He watched, barely breathing, as Karen walked to the front door and flung it open. "Yes?" she said.

A woman's voice said, "Hi, we're here for the interview; is Jordan ready? I'm sorry we're late, but this shouldn't take more than an hour or so." Mary Hart pushed her way past Karen, followed by a man in a suit and another with a camera perched like a pet bird on his shoulder, the crew from "Hollywood Dateline." "Hi, Jordan," Mary Hart said, raising her hand and waving. She smiled hugely and began walking toward him as he sunk into the cushions.

"Wait a minute," Karen said. "Mr. Manmouth is going to have to cancel . . ."

The man in the suit pointed the cameraman into position. "You, over there for the close-ups," he said.

Mary Hart fumbled under the blanket for Jordan's hand and began shaking it. "I want to thank you for the time today, Jordan. I'm a big fan of yours, you know. I love scary stories."

"I'm sorry," Karen said, trying to interfere, "but you . . ."

"Look," Jordan said. How had he forgotten about this? "I'm not really . . . Can we make it another . . . This isn't really the right . . ."

"Oh, I promise we'll be out of your hair in, oh, half an hour, maybe forty-five minutes. Cross my heart." She looked behind her for the producer.

"You want to do it outside?" the producer asked.

"No, no, this is great," Mary Hart said. "The horror writer at home, all bundled up and looking scared. I love it!"

"Look," Karen said. She walked up and grabbed Hart's shoulder. "I'm going to have to ask you to come back another time. He's sick."

Another guy had set up floodlights, and he switched them on, nearly blinding Jordan. The cameraman hefted his videocam into position. "We're ready here," he said.

"Great," the producer said. "Mary, you want to move in, and then we'll shoot the reverse?"

He couldn't do it, he thought. No matter how many times he'd smiled for the camera, today he just couldn't do it. "Look," he said.

All he saw was the huge eye of the camera; the tape was whirring.

"We're here today," Mary Hart began, and in the glass of the camera's lens Jordan saw his own face, and behind him, right behind the couch on which he sat, the hooded figure began to slip the cord . . .

Jordan screamed and pushed backwards with his feet, an involuntary movement of such force he sent the couch toppling. He sprawled on the floor, struggling with the blankets, gasping for breath. Somewhere far away he could hear someone screaming, someone who sounded like him.

"I told you, damnit," Karen yelled. "Get out of here now. Get the hell out of this house." There were sounds of a struggle. "Get out," Karen yelled.

"You get that?" the producer said.

"Every bit of it. Great stuff," the cameraman said.

"We'll run it tonight," the producer crowed. "The stations are gonna love this." More footsteps; Karen's voice raised in anger. Then they were gone.

Somehow she managed to get him upstairs. First she blindfolded him, then she monitored each step he took, until she'd locked the bedroom door behind her, latched the louvered doors to the bathroom, undressed him, and got him under the covers. He was shaking uncontrollably; he knew he'd completely lost his mind.

"Water," he said.

She brought him a glass of water and told him to close his eyes; then she gently sat him up and brought the water to his lips, cool, beautiful water in which he knew he could see his own reflection. He clamped his eyes so tight they hurt.

"Pills," she said. "Open your mouth; I want you to take these pills." He did as he was told.

"Now lie back," she said. "And rest. This will help you sleep. And tomorrow we're seeing a doctor." There it was, what he'd been expecting all afternoon. Who could blame her?

How had he gotten to this state? He was the one who frightened people, not the one who was frightened. They'd made him do it, they'd pushed him to this, his fans with their distorted faces and grabbing hands, his voracious, lascivious fans.

"You'll stay with me tonight, won't you?" he whispered. "You'll stay right here beside me?"

"Of course," she said. "Right here." He opened his eyes. Her face was beautiful, filled with sorrow. She lay down beside him and hugged him.

"I love you, Karen," he said.

"I love you too," she said.

He turned to face her. "I'm sorry about all this. I . . ."

"Shhhhh," she said and put a finger to his lips. And then she moved to kiss him. He closed his eyes, felt the warmth and tender pressure of her lips. For the first time since he'd been put in jail, he felt halfway human.

She pulled back and he took a deep breath, feeling the tension drain from him.

"Go to sleep," she said. "Everything will be fine tomorrow."

"I know," he said. He opened his eyes to look at her; she was very close, so close he could see his own reflection in her iris, and behind him, coming out of the bed itself, two black gloved hands slipped the garotte around his neck.

He was choking to death; he couldn't scream. Both his hands tried to pull the invisible cord away from his neck so he could get a breath, but the force was inhuman. He lunged upwards, but was pulled back. He thrashed on the bed in a paroxysm of terror and pain, as though he were being electrocuted.

Karen was on her knees, screaming. "Jordan!" she yelled. "God, Jordan, let me help you."

And then the pressure ceased. He looked at Karen; her hands covered her mouth and her eyes were wide in horror. He put his hands to his face and felt peeling skin, a black leather facemask, the flapping folds of a black hood.

"Noooooo!" he screamed, jumping to his feet. He was dressed in leather, and a cloak hung from his shoulders. "Nooo!" he screamed, tearing at his face.

Karen was shrieking now, wild hysterical shrieks that sounded like a police siren.

Jordan Manmouth bashed through the locked louvered doors into the bathroom. He ran to the mirror but knew what he would find. From somewhere he heard what sounded like laughter, applause, the tumultuous acclaim of a vast audience. His face was hideous, the unearthly white of a full moon in Los Angeles, and as wrinkled as a dessicated apple; shreds of skin fluttered from his cheeks. The face mask couldn't obscure who he was, and the black hood only worsened his pallor.

Karen was slumped against the louvered doors, screaming in terror. He turned to the French windows, through which the sound of wild applause was filtering. He gathered his strength and ran across the room, throwing himself through the window, into the arms of his invisible and adoring fans.

FINE TUNING
by Steven Bauer

Based on the Universal Television series *Amazing Stories*
Created by Steven Spielberg
Adapted from the episode ''Fine Tuning''
Teleplay by Earl Pomerantz
Story by Steven Spielberg

I'M NOT TOO GOOD AT SCHOOL, ALL THINGS CON-
sidered, and I'm worst at math and science if you
want to know the truth. So when Mr. Richards,
who's taught at my high school in Maywood since the
dawn of time, assigned group science projects, I
knew just what to do. I made a beeline for Andy
Slauson; so did my best friend Jimmy Cummings.

We called Andy "the Brain," and not for a lack of
other things to call him. He was tall, with straw-
blond hair and glasses and ballpoint pens in a plastic
case in his shirt pocket. He was kind of withdrawn,
always thinking; and even the teachers would yell at
him sometimes because they'd ask him a question
and he'd just be staring out the window. When *I* did
that, I was daydreaming—thinking about Denise

Jaynes, or about a hot fudge sundae, or about the Dodgers or the Rams—and if my father caught me "thinking," he'd always say, "Yeah, I thought I smelled wood burning."

But Andy Slauson was *really* thinking. For example, his mother wanted him to play the clarinet, and he hated it. She made him practice for fifteen minutes every day—*made* him, you understand. She closed him in his room and if she didn't hear his clarinet going, she'd yell at him from downstairs until she heard it again.

So Andy did this real smart thing—he made a tape of himself practicing, stopping, starting, making mistakes, squawking like a small animal caught in a trap. Mostly it was "My Country 'Tis of Thee." And then, whenever he had to go practice, he'd just punch the tape recorder's button and do something else which he found more interesting. Like work on our science project.

When the three of us first got together—Andy a little teed off at me and Jimmy, because he *knew* what we wanted, but glad just the same, I think, to get the attention—we talked about what we might do. Jimmy and I just repeated all the stuff we'd ever heard about science fairs, like hatching chickens or boiling the meat off a dead cat and putting the skeleton together. Then we got creative; Jimmy mentioned making a bomb, maybe, and I thought about how to see into girls' bedrooms so they couldn't see me.

But Andy wanted to work with electronics; he wanted to build a homemade TV antenna strong enough to pull in signals from far away. Like Sacramento or Oakland, about five hundred miles or so from where we were in the Los Angeles area. And he was "the Brain."

Now if I could explain to you how one of those

things worked, I wouldn't have needed Andy Slauson to drag me through my sophomore science class. I always thought of it like this: There was a place not far from where we lived where they sent out the pictures, exact copies of what you see when you turn on the tube, except ultra-teeny.

And these pictures which you couldn't see *at all* went zipping through the air until they hit those antennas on peoples' houses. This explained why some rooftops looked like small junk heaps—the more arms and legs, the better the chance of catching a teeny picture. All you needed was to catch one and it would slide down the metal and into your set. When you used rabbit ears, you wouldn't get as clear a picture as from the roof; the little teensy pictures had to bash their way through wood, glass, or reinforced concrete. I mean, they really had to *want* to get to you if all you had was rabbit ears.

Of course, Andy Slauson thought my idea was a riot. He tried to explain how it really happened— waves and dots and stuff like that—but I just tuned him out. If he wanted to build his own antenna, that was fine with me as long as it had my name on it too. I tried to convince him to go for Oakland instead of Sacramento. If you've ever been to Sacramento, you know why.

When I first saw it, I couldn't believe it. The two "ears" were made of clothes hangers, and they really would have looked like ears if we'd stretched old white socks over them like I wanted to. These were attached to a metal box which had wires inside, and a metal wheel with teeth for turning. I slapped my forehead when I saw it; I couldn't afford a D in science, considering my grades in math and English.

So I was halfway thinking of talking to Mr. Richards and seeing if I could get switched to Elisa

Pritchard's group when Andy cornered me and Jimmy in the hall and told us he'd got China.

"I was just fiddling around," he said, "and my Mom was calling me for dinner. I played with the fine tuning and there was this basketball game on and the guy says"—here he changed his voice—" 'This is KDPH, the home of Idaho basketball.' " I looked at Jimmy and Jimmy looked at me. "So anyway," he said, "I readjusted the thing and there's this fat guy in a huge flowered shirt, and he's wearing one of those necklaces and there are palm trees in the background. And *he* says, 'If you can find a better deal than right here at Kaiahuna Cars, I will personally eat a pineapple.' " Then Andy's eyes darted around like he was about to tell secrets to the Russians. "Get it?" he said. "Hawaii."

Jimmy starts swaying his hips and waving his arms like he's a native dancer. Then Andy said, "Next I got China. You wouldn't believe it. I know what the weather's like in Beijing. My antenna really works."

"Hey," I said. "*Our* antenna, Brain. You keep forgetting it's a team project."

"That's because you weren't helping."

"You threw us out of your house," I said.

"Because you weren't helping, George," Andy said.

Now you know why people call him names.

"You think *you're* helping with this China stuff? You probably got China*town*," I said. "We're all gonna flunk."

"Hey, this is the *Brain*," Jimmy said. He'd stopped the native dancing when Bridget Farbunkle pointed at him and started laughing. "If he says China, I believe him."

Andy relaxed for the first time since we'd been talking; I guess he spent his whole life waiting for people to make fun of him. "If you want," he said, "you could come over to my house tonight and see for yourselves."

"I don't know," I said. "I checked the listings and there's nothing good on in China." I was a funny guy.

Well, we went, of course. Mrs. Slauson always gave us Cokes and taco chips, and all Jimmy and me had to do was fool around while Andy got stern and lectured us. Jimmy and I were ready for anything when Andy started messing with the fine tuning.

The screen looked like Buffalo in January: snow, snow, snow.

"Wow, would you look at that?" I said.

"Amazing," Jimmy said. "Now I see why we reopened relations with the Orient."

"It worked yesterday," Andy said.

"Here, let me try," I said, and made a grab for the clothes hangers. Andy stopped me.

"Get your hands off," Andy said.

"It's a team project," I said. "The least you can do is let me touch it." This time I pushed him aside and got a hold on the antenna. We struggled a bit; we were bending the rabbit ears and breathing hard when suddenly Jimmy said, "Freeze."

We stopped and dropped our hands and backed away from the tube. Even though it was fuzzy, there was a picture. Andy played with the tuning and suddenly the reception was perfect. At first I thought it was "Sesame Street" because the two figures were all dressed up in weird costumes. It looked like they had wooden hands and rollers on their feet; they slid instead of walked. One of them was wearing a fright wig and a print dress; the other had on a fifties suit with big shoulders. Both of them looked as though they'd never worn clothes like that before. When they talked, it was all jumbled up like static, and then they'd stop, as if they were waiting for a laugh track, and there was the sound of pieces of wood being hit together.

"What *is* this?" I said. I'd come to the conclusion it wasn't "Sesame Street" or even a special. I mean, it was *weird*.

"It's not from China," Andy said.

"It's not from Earth," Jimmy said. That cracked me up. But Andy just said "Wow" real soft, under his breath, and stared at the TV screen. We shut up because the Brain was thinking. "You know what this is?" he said. "It's a signal from another planet." Jimmy and I looked at each other; Jimmy raised his eyebrows. I was about to make *Twilight Zone* noises.

"Who knows how strong this antenna is?" Andy said. "If it could pick up China . . ."

"If you're right," I said, "it's a sure A."

But Jimmy was suddenly watching the screen as though he was beginning to believe it might be true, and I stopped my joking around. "The way I figure it," Andy said, "the closest sun that could support a solar system like ours is ten light-years away. This signal was transmitted from some planet, like ten years ago."

"Reruns from outer space," Jimmy said. Now Jimmy is a TV fanatic, but this was too much for me. I mean, the kid would watch *any*thing. On the screen, the two figures were sliding around in a circle; the one in the suit said something like "loo see" and then fired a bunch of weird words at the one in the dress. She put her wooden hands on her head and started to make a noise like "boo hoo hoo" and then she wailed, "Oh Ree Key."

"I think they're doing *I Love Lucy*," Jimmy said. "I've seen this episode a million times. Watch, here come the Mertzes. Their furnace just blew up."

I stared at the screen; the door opened and two

more sliding figures came in covered completely with soot. There was a fadeout followed by a big lacy valentine with some weird writing in the middle; sure enough, there was the theme music—*Do do do, do-do duh, do-do*—played on alien instruments.

"We're getting their transmission from ten years ago," Andy said. "They must have gotten ours from twenty. Or more."

"This is incredible," Jimmy said. "What's on next?"

"I lost the *TV Space Guide*," I said. "Got any Nachos?"

Three hours later we were still there; Jimmy and I had called home to tell our parents we were about to make a real breakthrough on our science project, and Mr. and Mrs. Slauson said we could sleep over. On the screen an alien man with a big cigar was talking with an alien woman in front of a tall curtain. The clue had been "gray sea," but Jimmy didn't need a clue. It was Burns and Allen, and Jimmy was translating.

" 'How's your cousin Arthur?' " Jimmy said, doing George Burns. " 'Oh,' " he said, doing Gracie. " 'Cousin Arthur has three feet.' " The George Burns alien took the cigar out of its mouth. " 'Gracie, your cousin Arthur has three feet?' " Jimmy said. The Gracie alien said, " 'I got a letter from Aunt Rose saying Arthur had grown another foot.' " From the soundtrack came that clacking noise.

"Six shows," Andy said. "Six rip-offs. Why don't they make up their own shows?"

"Maybe they're not a funny planet," I said.

We were getting ready to call it one weird night when dot matrix letters started looping across the screen. We couldn't read them, of course, but there was a sudden cut to what looked like a fifties news desk. The alien was babbling while a picture showed these three figures heavily bundled in quilts. They had fishbowls on their heads.

"Astronauts," Andy said.

"I wonder where they're going," Jimmy said.

The news alien held up a globe of the earth and spun it, stopped it on North America. And then through a series of quick zooms it zeroed in on the western U.S., California, southern California, Los Angeles.

"Oh my God," I said. "They're coming here." Then there were stills of the Hollywood sign, the Chinese Theater, the footprints in the cement, and the corner of Hollywood and Vine. "Everyone comes here," I said. "Why can't somebody exercise a little imagination and go somewhere *else*?" Then there were shots of all these people who looked vaguely familiar.

Jimmy ticked them off, one by one. "Lucille Ball, Phil Silvers, Jackie Gleason, Art Carney, Milton Berle."

"Maybe they're coming down to get autographs," I said. Jimmy and Andy were staring at the screen like it was World War III or something; I wanted to lighten it up.

"I think you're right," Jimmy said. "When do you think they'll get here?"

"I don't know," Andy said. "It's taken at least ten years for these signals to arrive. If they took *off* ten years ago, and if they were able to travel at the speed of light, we'd have to know the exact date . . ."

"We do," I said. The screen flashed *April 23, 1976*.

"God," Andy said. "They've even measured *time* according to us."

"And they're landing next Tuesday," Jimmy said.

"What are we going to do?" He was right, of course; we were having visitors, and we weren't prepared.

On Tuesday we all skipped school and hung around on Hollywood and Vine. We didn't tell anyone, because who'd believe *us*? I was skittery as a spider on a griddle; Jimmy wore dark glasses and tried to act cool. Andy had his clarinet; we'd figured if music had worked in *Close Encounters* it would work for us.

The trouble was that *everyone* looked like he'd come from another planet. A real tall, skinny woman with a shaved head and leopard-skin tights had just been delivered by the Starship *Enterprise*. A man in his seventies wore baggy leather bermudas, and his wife had her hair done up in spirals and curls as if to catch radio waves. And then there were all the punkers with no eyebrows and hoops through their noses and spiked hair and makeup. I mean, who could tell the real aliens from the fake ones?

We looked everywhere; we combed the street together and apart. And we'd come back together, discouraged and exhausted, when I saw three guys browsing at a newsstand, all about five feet tall wearing long gray overcoats and matching gray fedoras, with fake bushy eyebrows and plastic noses and unlit cigars sticking out of their faces.

Three Groucho imitations.

One of them reached for a *TV Guide*—and his hand was wood.

"Guys," I said. "We found them."

With a look of interplanetary importance on his face, Andy dropped to the sidewalk, opened his case, and assembled his clarinet. With him in the lead, the three of us edged closer to the Grouchos, but they saw us coming and started buzzing in that language we'd heard on the tube, pointing to the clarinet as though it were a strange weapon.

"Do not be afraid," I said loudly, speaking as clear as I could. I mean, I figured they had to know English, but the words didn't seem to make sense to them.

"Lucy," Jimmy said, and their eyebrows stopped flapping.

"Gracie," I said.

Andy brought the clarinet to his lips and squawked out the mother ship's melody from *Close Encounters*. All three of the Grouchos put their hands to their mouths and shrugged, as if they didn't know what Andy was doing. Then Andy played three notes —the second higher than the first, the third between the other two.

The aliens clapped their wooden hands together —the clacking from the sound track we'd heard —and bustled toward us, the welcoming committee they hadn't expected.

"What was that?" I said to Jimmy.

"They don't know movies, only TV," he said. "That was an old TV signal. NBC. Whammo! We just made contact."

Well, at *my* house when someone drops over for a visit my folks give them something to eat. And these guys, after all, had been on the go for ten years. So we took them to a coffee shop.

Since they didn't speak the language, we ordered for them—a good old American meal, hamburgers and Cokes all around. The waitress brought the burgers, but not before the conversation had gotten a little difficult. I mean, these guys were pretty nice, but it's hard when all you have at your disposal is "You Bet Your Life" and "Say good-night, Gracie."

The Grouchos looked at their plates and their

glasses and it was clear they needed help. "Here, do it like this," I said. I unwrapped my straw and sucked up some Coke. The Grouchos made little murmuring noises; they fumbled with their straws (wooden fingers must be a pain) and then made up for lost time; they extended these snouts from their faces, like vacuum cleaner hoses, placed them in the glasses, and in an instant their Cokes were gone.

"They were thirsty," Jimmy said. "Good thing we ordered the large."

Then we showed them about burgers; Jimmy and Andy and I put mustard, catsup, and relish on ours, and the Grouchos followed suit, adding sugar, pepper, and Sweet 'n Low. I guess they didn't really understand. But they seemed to like them fine. Again their snouts lowered to their plates, and in one quick intake of breath they were gone, utterly, sucked inside by their huge and powerful interior vacs.

"We're gonna need more burgers," Andy said. "These guys look hungry enough to eat a horse."

All three of the Grouchos froze; then one turned to Andy and said what sounded like "horse." In quick succession the other two said "horse" and both Jimmy and I said "horse." Suddenly, we were making progress. Everyone at the table could say *horse*.

Then one of the Grouchos said, "Lid lull jo."

Andy and I were clueless; we turned to Jimmy. "Horse," he said. "Lid lull jo." Then a beatific look of comprehension crossed his face. "Bonanza!" he said.

"Bonanza!" the three Grouchos said.

"Adam, Ben," Jimmy said.

"Bonanza!" the three Grouchos said.

Like fraternity brothers repeating the magic word, all four of them yelled "Ponderosa!" And holding wooden hands (except, of course, for Jimmy) they launched into a perfectly rhythmic but toneless rendition of the theme song: you know—the one that goes *dun da-da dun-dun da-da-da-da dun* BONANZA! Andy and I joined in on the last word.

Because they were polite aliens, they felt they owed *us* a treat after the burgers, so they took us to their spaceship. Inside we found a sort of shrine, the center of which was a strange TV, not at all like anything I'd ever seen on earth; it seemed to play, nonstop, American shows from the fifties and early sixties. When we entered, Larry, Moe, and Curley were hitting each other with bricks and boards and banana cream pies. Our friends put on Three Stooges wigs and imitated their antics, pantomiming, thank God, the bricks, boards, and pies. "I can't believe it," I said. "I'm on a spaceship."

"They must really trust us to bring us here," Andy said.

"We must really trust *them*," Jimmy said, "to come."

It was our turn again, so we took them where we knew they'd most want to go—the Green Line Tour, "The Homes of the Stars." By this time our paranoia had been whittled away almost to nothing; no one had noticed the aliens inhaling food and drink in a Hollywood coffee shop, and we'd walked the streets without getting more than the usual number of stares.

Still, I was a little uneasy because it had occurred to me you didn't travel ten years at the speed of light in order to eat a burger. So they wanted something else, but we didn't know what. And after seeing *V: The Series* I was hoping it wasn't anything else in the food department.

They'd taken off their Groucho disguises and now looked like tourists—straw hats, sport jackets made of metallic cloth, plaid pants, white socks. Their faces, you understand, didn't look like tourists' faces; they didn't look like *human* faces. They had round eyes and no eyebrows and where the nose should be was this expandable tube, like I said. Their mouths fell easily into a perfect imitation of the letter *O*. Not pretty to look at, in other words, but they seemed to have good hearts (or something similar) and there was an age and wisdom to their eyes which made them look very kind. And besides, we'd all been brought up not to stare at freaks.

We drove slowly along the expansive tree-lined streets of Beverly Hills, and our friends clung by their wooden fingers to the bus's windows. Andy was scouring a map of "The Homes of the Stars" and together with the driver's sonorous voice, was keeping our visitors informed.

Then we passed this old guy.

He was out jogging. He wore a sweat-stained gray tee-shirt and a pair of white tennis shorts; around his head was a terrycloth sweatband, and he was huffing and puffing along. A ripple of *ooohs* passed through the bus. Our friends went crazy, acting like clips of girls at early Beatles concerts, screaming, jumping around, fainting, being fanned back to consciousness.

"What's going on?" I said.

"That's Milton Berle," Jimmy said. "One of the biggest comedy stars TV ever had."

"I think they know his work," Andy said.

The guy called Berle waved to the bus, but he was sweating pretty heavily by now, and didn't put forth too much effort.

I was real happy we'd managed to show our new friends an honest-to-God celebrity, even if I didn't know who he was, but when I turned to them, they weren't in their seats. In fact, they'd vanished from the bus.

We looked out the window and there they were,

running after Milton Berle.

Although this sort of thing just isn't done, we made the driver stop. It was pretty funny, I guess, if you were still on the bus: there's this Berle guy, and then these three outlandish-looking weirdos and then the three of us, normal American teenagers, if you let Andy pass for one, all running like in a race.

Milton Berle jogged up to his front door and bent over, breathing hard, checking his pulse. When he looked up, the six of us were standing there, in a big semicircle. "Yes?" he said.

It was real silent for a minute or two, then Jimmy speaks up. "They don't mean to bother you, Mr. Berle. They're just real big fans of yours and they . . ."

"What do they want?" Berle asked. "Autographs?"

Now as far as I was concerned, this was the big question. What *did* they want?

Our friends were swooning—I can't think of a better word—twisting their hands together and rolling their little eyes around, awe and admiration on their faces.

"Anybody got a pen?" Berle asked.

The guys huddled together now, and when they broke out, they were a lot more composed, even sedate. One of them stepped forward and earnestly talked at Berle who looked thoroughly bewildered. I didn't know for sure, but the tone of the guy's voice made it sound like a business proposition.

Berle listened politely, then said, "I didn't get any of that."

"It's French," I said, and Andy elbowed me.

"No it's not," said Berle. The one who'd just spoken held out his empty wooden hands in unmistakable entreaty. The others slid up and grabbed

Berle's two arms and tried to move him away from his door.

"What's going on?" Berle said "What do they want? And why are they so short?"

Then suddenly, like the old lightbulb going on in the cartoons, I understood. They were tired of all the original shows they'd seen and seen, tired of their own loony copies; they wanted the real authentic thing, and they'd come down to get it.

"Hello, boys," Milton Berle said. "Are these friends of yours?"

"Well," Andy said, "you see, they're from out of town."

"How *far* out of town?" Berle said, staring down at the guys.

"*Very* far," I said. "You wouldn't believe how far. It's kind of hard to explain. See, they really love the TV shows you used to make, and they were hoping you'd go back with them and make some more."

"Go back to where?" Berle asked. "Would I have artistic control? What's my time slot? Who am I on against? Who's my sponsor? I need particulars."

While two of them started wildly pantomiming —fast cars, shapely women, lots of bucks—the third stepped forward with a big fat cigar. Berle lit it speculatively and made a face. "Where *is* this place?" he said. "Forget it. I can't work in a place that doesn't have a decent cigar."

Then, in perfect imitation of their dialect, Berle stepped up to the three and explained the situation, shaking his head no the whole time. They dropped their heads to their chests, the poor guys; I've never seen such hangdog looks. It was enough to break your heart.

Well, we had to do something to relieve their misery, especially when they finally understood that

Lucy and Desi had split up and wouldn't be getting back together. So we found them some talent eager and ready to make the trip . . .

> Q: *Would you hit a lady with a baby?*
> A: *No. I'd hit her with a brick.*

> Person # 1: *Well, well, well . . .*
> Person # 2: *If all these wells come in, we'll be rich.*

They were old vaudevilleans, from Andy's grandfather's Senior Citizens center, and they were as willing to go as the old people in *Cocoon* had been. They were delighted to have an audience, and the ecstatic faces of our three friends made us think we'd really contributed to interplanetary understanding. Everyone was pleased as punch, and you can't knock a happy ending. We watched them take off, and though we got a little sentimental (after all, they were *our* aliens) we thought they'd be back. I mean, old vaudeville can get tiresome after a while.

Well, it was *almost* a happy ending: Mr. Richards liked our project pretty well but didn't believe Jimmy and I had helped. He gave Andy an A, but Jimmy and me, we got Bs.

And the day we brought the TV to school to show the class, we only reached as far as Sacramento. Of course, since I'd bet my allowance clear through August that we'd get at least to Honduras, I was pretty poor for the next few months.

But I still think of those guys from time to time, wonder what they're watching on TV. I mean, I'd really like to see an alien version of *Dynasty*, know what I mean? The real Joan Collins is already pretty much an alien, in my book at least. And what would they think of Kit in *Knight Rider?* Do they have talking vehicles on their planet? Or maybe they only like comedy. How about a Sam and Diane with wooden hands? *Give Me A Break!*

REMOTE CONTROL MAN
by Steven Bauer

Based on the Universal Television series *Amazing Stories*
Created by Steven Spielberg
Adapted from the episode ''Remote Control Man''
Teleplay by Douglas Lloyd McIntosh
Story by Steven Spielberg

YOU ARE DRIVING DURING RUSH HOUR, AS YOU DO every day, down the Ventura Freeway. Although you've rolled up the windows, the blue exhaust of the hurtling cars around you fills the old beat-up Ford you're driving; every now and then you cast an envious glance at one of those small jazzy foreign cars —with names like Isuzu and Mitsubishi, names that fill you with a longing for travel, anything to remove you from this rut you're in—but you can't look for long because they're gone, zipping by you in the passing lanes as you trudge along, horns blaring behind you, at the poor excuse for speed the Ford can manage.

In a rut: you even listen to the same music every drive home, the same classical station which always plays Vivaldi. In fact, you're half-convinced it al-

ways plays the *same* Vivaldi, but you're so unsavvy
about music, you're unwilling to mention this peculiar fact to anyone.

But it's not just the drive, the exhaust, the
music—it's what lies ahead tonight and tomorrow.
First, the attack of the killer dachshunds; then the
abuse of Grendel, your wife, a woman who, unaccountably and because it's your fault (she's told you
so), has let herself go, if "letting oneself go" can
describe, in fact, what's happened to her.

You'll undoubtedly as well be forced to see your
two sons, Bill, the older, a Hare Krishna who, despite
the fact he's adopted the name Maheshswara along
with his saffron robes and shaved head, hasn't given
up his addictions to Velveeta, fried pork rinds, or
Gatorade. And Ralph, who at eleven might as well
have been enrolled for the last year in the Charlie
Manson School of Etiquette. With his spiked orange
hair, the diaper pin through his nose, and those tee-
shirts he wears, he looks as though he's someone you
might see on *Entertainment Tonight*, plugging a
video—not someone you'd see in your living room,
in the flesh. When the interviewer asks him what he
wants to do when he "grows up," he'll reply, "Oh, I
dunno. Kill the President."

But at least there's your TV. It's Wednesday night
and *Highway to Heaven*'s on; maybe Michael Landon (who you've always liked, since *Bonanza*, and all
through *Little House*) will materialize in your living
room and say, "I'm an angel, and I'm going to help
you." Maybe. But doubtful.

Then troubled sleep, and tomorrow and tomorrow
and tomorrow . . .

Well, it won't do to think about work. Better to
think about that fiendish woman in the red Camaro
who's bearing down on you as though all she's ever
wanted is to rear-end someone. The Vivaldi hurries
along, all sunshine, as you stare in the rearview, see-

ing yourself—Walter Poindexter, forty-seven, balding, bespectacled, scared to death—chasing a certain
future, as certain as the exit ahead which you almost,
almost miss.

As always, you cut the engine and the Vivaldi, and
coast the last quarter mile—it's downhill, and perhaps you can fool the dachshunds. You pull the car
in front of your curb, since the driveway—for the
dogs—is a certain clue. You slump a little, survey the
bushes through slitted eyes. From the back seat you
take the trash can lid you carry with you. Then,
clutching the lid in one hand, your briefcase in the
other, you begin creeping across your spotty brown
lawn toward that pink depressing house with its green
shingles and shutters.

Your house.

You think you've fooled them today, those savage
sausages on legs, when you hear the gathering shrieks
of their wild pack. Out of nowhere, they beseige you,
their nickety little teeth snapping and nipping at your
pants. Dragging them along, kicking out at them as
though they were something unfortunately attached
to the tip of your shoe (and they are), you finally,
desperately, manage to enter your living room, leaving them scratching and yipping in your wake.

Home sweet home. You breathe a sigh of relief,
then look around as you always do, in hopes you've
entered a changed house. This one is disturbing; the
sofa is covered with worn turquoise vinyl, and all the
furniture—the easy chair you call yours, the battered
Formica coffee table—stand on spindly wooden legs.
As you stash the garbage can lid in the front closet,
Grendel's voice calls from the kitchen.

Screeches, actually. *"Walter!"* You wipe a sleeve
across your forehead and call out meekly, "Yes,
dumpling?" She *does* look like a dumpling, like a
kreplach, but you have little time to ponder similes,

for she screeches, "Get in here."

What domestic bliss and harmony meet your eyes as you enter your kitchen! Grendel, with a sweet smile, beckons you to come to the stove where she's making your favorite dessert, and she wants you to lick the chocolate frosting from her . . .

Actually, Grendel sits at the kitchen table in training to become a Sumo wrestler. She weighs, oh, two hundred ten pounds, and looks as though she's just gotten out of bed. Her robe is dirty, as is her hair which is still in curlers, and on the floor, her feet in their fuzzy little slippers look like epileptic bunnies as they skitter on the linoleum. She has taken time from reading the tabloids and eating a gallon of ice cream to yell at you.

"Where is it?" she says.

"It?" you ask, stalling for time.

She holds up the empty cardboard bucket into which she's been jabbing a large aluminum spoon and says, "My Tutti Spumoni! I'm sick and tired of Heavenly Hash!"

"I'm sorry, Peaches," you say, but she throws the carton across the room and snarls, "Sorry excuse for a husband is what you are."

Perhaps you can make it up to her; perhaps you can placate her. "Is there anything else I can do for you, dear?"

"Yeah," she says. "There's a spoon in the garbage disposal. Get it out."

Something about garbage disposals has always frightened you—the slime of pureed food, the sharp little blades like dachschund teeth, the dark where you can't really see—but you resolutely put your briefcase down, take off your jacket, loosen your tie, and roll up your sleeves. This is man's work.

You're massaging last night's dinner, trying to grasp the spoon, as Grendel says dreamily, "I wanna go to Cypress Point in Florida this summer. They got a fountain of youth I wanna check out.'' Just the ticket for old Grendel, you think, when you hear footsteps.

It's Ralph with his murderous grin, his spiked hair, his Rats on Fire tee-shirt. "Hi there, son," you say, trying to hide what you're doing from him, for you know, sure as God made little white toadstools, that Ralph is on his way to the garbage disposal switch.

Your hand, of course, is stuck; that little rubber ring has it tight as a manacle. Feet braced against the baseboard, your free hand pushing against slippery Formica, you try with all your might to break loose as your fingers retract into your palm as though they were made to do that. Ralph hits the switch—you knew it was no joke—and lucky for you the vacuum is broken. Just as the machine is about to make finger food, your hand pops out like a champagne cork.

Now what would most men do in such a situation? Like them, you reach for your son, in order to exert pressure around his throat so as to render breathing difficult. But his protector, his bodyguard, his great bear of a mother is on you before you can kill him: "Lay a hand on that poor little boy and I'll smother you in your sleep.''

Such sweetness! Such kindness! Such understanding!

"That 'poor' little boy just tried to grind off my hand in the garbage disposal,'' you say indignantly.

But obviously, you haven't been reading the latest books on child psychology, for the offended mother says, "Don't you know a cry for love when you hear one?''

Taking his cue, your youngest sobs into his mother's overt and heaving bosom. "Daddy hates me!'' he says.

"Don't worry, sweetums," Grendel says. "Mommy's here."

Shall we complicate the scene? Shall Bill, a.k.a. Maheshswara, your older son, enter now and say, "There is no inner harmony here, no oneness with the cosmos. We must manifest the selfness that suffuses the internal flow and lets peace and interior space pervade our beings." His hands are together as if in prayer; when they separate, one goes toward a cabinet and he says, "Where's the Velveeta?"

"Your father forgot to go to the store," Grendel says.

"Where's the Bac-O Bits?" Maheshswara says. "Where's the Cheese Doodles?" Though you apologize and call him by his new name he merely mutters, "Pathetic," and leaves the kitchen, shaking his head.

At eight P.M. you enter the den, switch on the old TV set, settle in your easy chair, ignore the turquoise vinyl, and sure enough, it's *Highway to Heaven*. There's Michael Landon, a little pudgy of face, with a bit too much hair and that annoying cleft in his chin (as an angel, it's hard not to look smug). Still, you grew up with him and his brothers Adam and Hoss; suddenly you wonder what Lorne Green would do with Maheshswara.

You're being lulled into another world when the air tenses behind you. "Oh, that's right," Grendel says. "Go to your precious TV. Run to never-never land and shut us out. You can't relate, Walter. For all you know, one of your sons could be a Mozart or a Shakespeare or a Lincoln or a Churchill."

"Or Attila the Hun," you say under your breath.

"What?" she shrieks. "What did you say?"

"I said, 'You're right, hon,' " you say.

•　　•　　•

Work. Let's see. How to describe? It begins in an office you've only heard about, a spacious office with curtains and a large desk and a small outer room containing a blonde woman with polished nails and a very cute telephone voice. This is the main office of Beasley Manufacturing, a large building surrounded by chainlink fence; to someone on the outside it looks like San Quentin.

In this main office, Mr. Beasley himself pushes a button and a man appears. Mr. Beasley says, "I want those control graphs, and I want them now. And if I don't have them now, you're history." The man seems to understand this last odd phrase and says, "Yes sir, Mr. Beasley. Right away."

He walks, grim and determined, down a line of glass-partitioned offices, opens one door without knocking, and says, "We need these control graphs, and we need them now. And if we don't have them now, you're history." The man to whom they've been given says to another man, ". . . and if I don't get them right away, you're a memory." By the time the work reaches you, the threat has escalated. The beast who brings them to you says, "Do these now or you're dead."

Valium, anyone?

That night, as a ground fog creeps around the wheels of your car—it's after dark; those graphs took most of the afternoon, and the piles of work on your desk, well—you prepare for the attack of the killer dachshunds. You've made a dummy of yourself, a Walter Poindexter with even fewer bones. It's attached to a stick, and the dumb animals *go* for it, ripping off its pants, tearing at its tie. Safely inside, you peek out the window to see them devouring its head. For a moment you pride yourself on your ingenuity when you hear . . .

"Wal*ter*?"

You turn, and Grendel enters, looking like one of the rhinos from *Fantasia*. She's wearing a mini-skirt which reveals to the naked eye two legs like tree trunks; the feet are encased in stiletto-heeled pumps. She's wearing a platinum wig and eye makeup sufficient for most of Ventura County. As she twirls before you, she says, "What do you think?"

What you think is "Be very careful now, Walter." What you *say* is "Very nice, dumpling."

"Still a size nine," your wife exults. "And the whole outfit only cost $85."

"Where on earth did you get . . ."

And then you realize the TV is missing: where it used to sit, that shrine to fantasy, a somewhat darker square of carpet and a larger than usual number of dustballs are visible.

Now *you're* shrieking. "My television! What happened to my television?"

"I sold it," Grendel says. "How do you think I paid for the pumps?"

"That was my set," you say. "You had no right."

"That TV was ruining our sex life," she says.

You're not standing for this. Regardless of the dachshunds who undoubtedly wait just outside, you jerk open the door and run to your car, pursued by elongated beasties.

Inside, you push down the locks and start the engine, glancing from time to time at the enormous mini-skirted phantasm wobbling through the fog. Its wig is askew, its face crimson and contorted, its pudgy fists striking out at the droplets of water in the air. Before it can reach you, you leave it and the curb behind.

And cruise.

Driving in the fog is both difficult and luxurious; you can't quite see where you're going, but somehow it doesn't matter. Enveloped in a privacy you rarely experience, you coast along, looking for a store that sells TVs, driving up and down the unnamed streets, into a part of town you've never been before. Almost the moment you think it would be nice to find an appliance store, lights materialize, bluish lights which draw you to them. The large odd neon sign reads METALUNA DISCOUNT CENTER; on the window in hand-painted letters are the words "Unearthly Bargains: We'll Give You a Deal That's Out of This World."

Pretty terrific, you think, as you turn the car into the totally empty parking lot. You push open the door and enter. It's a large store, stocked with an array of stereo speakers, turntables, compact disk players, large-screen TVs, as well as washing machines, irons, and humidifiers; everything, in fact. But you're the only human among all these appliances, and you get a little nervous until a salesman, slim, dressed in gray, his hands clasped before him like a funeral director's, steps forward—out of *no*where—and says, "May I help you, Mr. Poindexter?" Are you wearing a name tag? You look down swiftly at your lapel, blushing, but there's no name visible, at least to you.

"I'd like to . . . uh . . . see a . . ."

"A television set, of course," the man says. "I have something just for you." You follow him to a console where he says, "It's an excellent set, quite unique. Nineteen-inch screen, diagonally measured, with the patented Magic Touch Remote Control."

"It looks expensive," you say.

"Tish tosh, Mr. Poindexter. Your credit is good here. Shall I load it into your car?"

"Sure," you say. "But how did you know my name?"

"We make it a point," the man says, "to know our prospective customers."

•　　•　　•

When you carry it into the living room, unbox it, and set it in place, you can't believe how happy you are: It's a real beauty. You turn it on, take your remote control, and sit in your easy chair. A quick inspection reveals the two crucial features of your new toy: The red button is the on/off switch; the bright blue button changes channels. You hit the red button and the screen instantly reveals an old black and white movie; you hit the blue button and see Ozzie Nelson earnestly talking to Harriet. You hit the blue button again and a ballerina *en point* is moving across an empty stage. Behind you, Grendel suddenly looms, in robe and slippers, still wearing the wig.

"Where'd you get that?" she screeches.

"I bought it," you say.

"With what?"

"Credit," you say.

Then she explodes. "So you've been holding out on me, you low-down lying louse. I slave day and night, working my fingers to the bone, and what do you pull—a private bank account."

"You don't understand, dumpling," you say. But she charges out of the room in fury, just as a touch of the blue button changes the channel to the Miss Teenage America Contest.

They're down to five finalists, in bathing suits, shifting their weight from one sweet hip to the other. The emcee says, "Now please describe for all of us what characteristics define your ideal man." And you're all ears, of course, to see how you stack up.

Contestant number one smiles at the camera and says, "My ideal man must be loving and warm and share my lifelong dream of a world at peace." So far, so good, you think.

A rumble behind you lets you know your loving spouse has returned; and you shift your gaze to discover . . .

She's coming at you, *and she's got an axe upraised*

in her hands. But she passes you by for the moment, on her way to the TV. "Turn it off!" she yells. "Turn it off or I swear I'll pulverize it. And you're next."

In desperation you press the red button, the on/off button. And Grendel and her axe both disappear.

How do you feel? Is this something you'd expected? Astonished, you walk to where Grendel was last seen, wave your hands through the air, step back, and push the red button again. There she is, bigger than life, and she's screaming, "It goes back tomorrow, you sniveling little rat. You contemp—"

You try to hit the red button to turn her off again, but you miss and hit the blue. And in Grendel's place is the beauty contestant you'd previously seen who says, "My ideal man would have a wonderful sense of humor because I want to spend all my time with him, all day and all night." Your jaw unhinges, hits your solar plexus. "To cook for him, clean for him, listen to him. And I'd know who he was, my Prince Charming, the minute he kissed me."

You look around the room. "Me?" you say.

"Just once," she says, closing her eyes, tilting her head back.

On tiptoes, about to plunge into extramarital bliss, you close *your* eyes, but just at that moment Maheshswara enters the room and screams, "MOTHER."

You point the remote at him and press the blue button, and lo and behold, the saffron-robed holy man becomes Dirk Benedict—Face—from *The A-Team*, swaggering, looking tough. "B.A.'s out buying earrings," he says. "The Colonel's buying cigars and Murdoch's out of his mind. So what about me? What do I get to be out of? This is supposed to be a team, an *equal* team. If *they're* out of something, *I'm* out of something." He shakes his head. "If anyone wants me, I'll be in tonight." And then he's gone.

Alone at last, you think. But not for long. There's Ralphie. Before he can utter a word, you press the blue button and *he's* transformed into Gary Coleman who says, "Whoa, Dad! I didn't know you were a player. Better get on the stick; I've got the soul sisters coming by in an hour and I'm gonna need the space." And then *he's* gone.

You kiss her; her lips are warm and pliant under yours. Your heart is beating fiercely. You give this kiss everything you've got.

"My knight in shining armor," she says. She's breathless. You? Well, you tell me.

In the morning, when you awake, you think, *What a pleasant dream*. Then you see the bathing suit. You sit up, yawn, stretch, rub your eyes, and sneak a peak at the wallow where Grendel usually is. But Grendel isn't there; in her place is Miss Teenage Arizona. She's beautiful, her face in repose, her bare shoulder and arm above the covers. You remember her words from TV: "To cook for him, clean for him, listen to him." Wake up, honey. Time for breakfast!

"Wake up," you say, nuzzling her cheek. "Rise and shine, you sexy contest winner."

She grumbles into wakefulness, glances at the clock, and says, "Yeah. Time to get jogging."

"But what about cooking my breakfast?" you say. "Remember what you said last night?"

She looks at you in open-mouthed wonderment. "Cook?" she says. "Me?"

Time for a change, you think, as you pick up the remote control from the bedside table and push the blue button. What luck! It's Barbara Billingsley, June Cleaver, wife to Ward, mother to Beaver and Wally, the all-around all-American Mom.

Dressed in a nightgown, she leaps from the bed. "Oh my goodness, Ward," she says. "I've never overslept in my life. I'm sorry, dear; breakfast in ten. Wally! Beaver! Time to get up or you'll be late for school!"

Breakfast is a bit odd. Not the food—bacon, scrambled eggs, muffins—but the company. It's not Wally and Beaver you sit down with, nor Bill and Ralphie. It's Dirk Benedict and Gary Coleman. Dirk is rattling on about women he's scored with, and Gary is as bright and disgustingly chipper as ever. But June Cleaver treats them as if they were old Wal and the Beav.

"Eat your eggs, Beaver," she says to Gary Coleman, "before they get cold. And you eat your eggs too, Wally." You wonder: Should she have said, "Eat your eggs Benedict?"

But Gary and Dirk aren't listening. "Hey, big guy," Coleman says to Benedict. "What say we ride up the coast, see if we can run game on a bevy of chicks."

"Sorry, kid," Benedict says. "I've got a date with a couple of felons."

It's time to interrupt, you think. "June, boys," you say, the head of this American family. "I've got something I want to say to you all . . . I just feel I have to . . . I have these other responsibilities . . . I hope you understand I just have to do this." You push the blue button, and everyone's back—Grendel, Maheshswara, and Ralphie, all in living, screaming Technicolor. You give them five seconds before you zap back your other family.

"Well, what's up, dad?" Gary asks.

"I just want to say that sitting here with you all, I feel like the luckiest man on the face of the earth."

● ● ●

Happiness like this can't continue, of course; it's one of the Laws of the Universe. Into every life, a little electronic snow must fall, and since you're Walter Poindexter, you're about to get more than your share.

You're at work, whistling, smiling, content for the first time in years. You're not even worried about the killer dachshunds. One push of the button and they'll be transformed into Lassies.

Then the telephone rings. It's June, and she sounds worried. "I'm sorry to disturb you at work, dear," she says, "but you'd better come home right away. Wally's in trouble."

She's right, of course. Inside the pink and green house she's tied back to back to Dirk Benedict; two hoodlums, in trench coats and fedoras, are holding them hostage. One picks his teeth with a switchblade; the other scratches his face with the snub-nosed barrel of his gun.

You want to know what's going on, and you ask.

"Nothing to get excited about, dad," Dirk says. "Everything's under control. Didn't happen to see the van outside, did you?"

"Torch the place, Vito," one of the thugs says, and Vito starts squirting the rug with lighter fluid.

"In my line of work," Dirk says, "there are times you've got to stand up to life's underbelly. A desperate widow asked for our help in smashing a loan-shark ring. But my cover's been blown and no one else on the A-Team knows about it. Can you help me out, dad?"

"Now, Ward," June says. "Wally's a *good* boy."

"Wreck the place, Vito," the switchblade says. As Vito approaches the TV with his heavy hobnail boots, you yell, "No! Not the TV! Anything but the TV!"

You point the r/c, push the the blue button, and

Vito becomes Richard Simmons chanting to disco
music, "Okay, super! For those slim-looking thighs,
we have to kick to the skies!"

"Hey," says the switchblade. "What's this?"

But Simmons tickles the thug's jaw with his shoe.
"For a tight little bun," he says, "you got to start
with a run."

You zap the remaining thug with your fingers
crossed, hoping he'll become someone nice—Mr.
Rogers, maybe, or Bill Cosby—but your luck's run
out. You've turned him into William Perry, The
Refrigerator himself, in his Chicago Bears uniform.

And he's coming right toward you, the top of his
head in his helmet like a battering ram. He hits
you—for a moment you can understand what it's like
to be a penny on a railroad track—and carries you
crashing through your dining room table. The remote
control flies from your hand, hits the wall, and slides
to the floor, cracked beyond repair. On the TV, stations roll wildly from one to another.

You've got nothing to say about it now: All the
demons of TV have been loosed, some friendly, some
not, some pretty, some not. Here comes Hulk
Hogan, in his sweatband and wrestling togs, with his
muscles and mustache and sneer. Here comes Jim
Lange, of *$100,000 Name That Tune*. The Hulk
wants to wrestle you, but Lange just wants you to
name that tune. Somewhere in the blurry background, Cyndi Lauper is dancing and swinging her
orange hair.

"You're garbage," the Hulk says. "I'm gonna
show you up for a wimp in front of twenty million
people . . ."

" 'Turkey in the Straw,' Walter," Lange says.
"You should have gotten that one."

It's not over yet. From the soaps, young ingenues
are caressing you, saying, "Anytime, anywhere,

anything!" and "I only married Joe because they threatened to kill you. I never slept with him, honest. I told him I was pregnant by you."

When Kit from *Knight Rider* comes crashing through your living room wall, you've had enough. "Help!" you scream. "Someone help me! Heeeeelllllp!"

Then *finally* there's Ed McMahon, friend to Johnny Carson, friend to late night viewers, friend to Publishers' Clearing House Sweepstakes, friend to you.

"Heeeeeeeeere's Walter!" he says.

"What am I gonna do, Ed?" you say, your hand on his shoulder. "Things have gotten out of control."

"What are you asking *me* for, Walter? I'm just a character on TV," Ed says. "I'm not the *real* Ed McMahon. I'm just shadows and light, light and shadows. Put your hand right through me. That's your problem, Walter," Ed continues. "You don't seem to be able to deal with the ups and downs of your life, so you escape to TV. But none of this is real."

Ed turns, as if to a studio audience, and says, "And now for our next guest, Clara Peller, the woman all America knows from her groundbreaking Wendy's commercials."

"All right, Walter," Clara says, striding on in her pugnacious and crotchety manner. "What's the beef?"

"He's got a problem," Ed McMahon says.

"I'm not even remotely in control," you say.

"You're a wimp," Clara says. "That's the trouble with you. You don't relate. You may think your wife and children are monsters, but maybe you've made them that way."

"Maybe you've made them that way," McMahon

says. "Maybe you were watching TV when you should have been spending time with them. Maybe you came home from work and tubed out every night."

"They think you're a wimp," Clara Peller says. "Watching the dumb game shows, dumb baseball games, dumb cop and doctor shows, dumb commercials."

"Why don't you tune us out, Walter?" McMahon asks.

"Yeah," Hulk Hogan bellows. "Turn us off."

"But I like TV," you say.

"Turn us off," June Cleaver says.

"Turn us off," Dirk Benedict says.

It's just no fun any more. The whole sick crew is chanting *Turn us off, turn us off*, as Richard Simmons kicks and shimmies, The Refrigerator tackles Clara Peller, Ed McMahon names that tune.

With your eyes closed, and your hands over your ears, you move toward the TV, and then, with a jab which carries with it your whole heart, you hit the OFF button with your knee.

And the room grows silent. You open your eyes. The car from *Knight Rider* is gone, the hole in the wall is gone, all gone, gone utterly: a terrible beauty is born.

You look around, stunned, at the turquoise vinyl, the Formica coffee table. And then you hear, from the direction of the bedroom, a familiar voice.

But it's different somehow, softer, more melodious, more tinged with regret than anger. It's not very strident at all, now that you listen. It's really a sweet voice, one you used to love. "Walter," she calls. "Please, for once, turn off the TV and come to bed. I'm lonely."

Could you have made it all up? The horror and the

fantasy? Could it have been a long waking dream in which you, so hermetically sealed in a TV world, were unable to see your wife and sons? Could that be? Still, you think wistfully of the night before, of Miss Teenage Arizona and those fingers of hers, those lips . . .

"Walter," Grendel calls. "I'm really asking you, honey. Come to bed."

Okay, you think. You shrug. You smirk. You do.

BOO
by Steven Bauer

Based on the Universal Television series *Amazing Stories*
Created by Steven Spielberg
Adapted from the episode ''Boo''
Teleplay by Lowell Ganz and Babaloo Mandel

THE CHUMSKEYS LIVED AT 3847 ELMWOOD DRIVE, the house they'd moved into when they'd married. It was a comfortable two-story house with an attic, on a street of houses not unlike theirs, with wood floors and plaster ceilings and a good-size back yard in which Evelyn Chumskey had planted roses, banks and banks of roses, which she'd tended happily every summer of her married life. Like them, the other families on the street were quiet, polite, and peaceful, families whose children were always riding bikes and running through sprinklers, playing tag and jump rope and kickball. On summer evenings, the smells of freshly mown grass and burning charcoal hung in the air like a benediction.

They were ghosts, the Chumskeys, though you wouldn't know it to look at them, if you'd been able to see them. They were what you'd call *nice* ghosts, fond of people, fond particularly of Richard and Barbara Tucker, and their children Scott and Deena. They were benevolent spirits, like guardian angels, and they watched over the current inhabitants of 3847 Elmwood Drive as though the Tuckers were members of their family. Which they were, of course.

But when, almost without warning, the Tuckers decided to move, the Chumskeys were rattled. Since their deaths, Nelson and Evelyn Chumskey had shared the place only with the Hunseckers and the Tuckers, lovely families, both of them. No telling who might move in next.

The night before the move, the Tuckers were in their bedroom, getting ready for bed. Richard Tucker was putting the last of his rolled-up socks in a large brown carton on which his wife had scrawled BEDROOM STUFF with a blue Magic Marker. Barbara was fluffing pillows, turning back the quilt. They fell on the bed exhausted and Richard turned and kissed his wife. He looked down at her inscrutable face and said, "Excited?"

"Couldn't be happier," Barbara said.

"And the new house? You really love it?"

"Hidden Valley Estates," Barbara said. "What's not to love? It's absolutely, positively, the most unbelievable . . ."

Richard kissed her again and when he drew back to smile at her, she was crying.

"Oh, sweetheart," he said helplessly.

"I'm sorry," Barbara said between sobs.

"It's going to be wonderful."

"I know, I know," she said. "It's just that this house . . ."

"We'll come to love it in Hidden Valley," Richard said.

"But all our friends . . ."

"We'll make tons of new ones." He paused until she'd stopped crying. "An hour a day on the freeway's been killing me," he said. "I never see you, I never see the kids."

She was wiping her face with a pillow. "I know, Richard, I do, and I'm sorry. There are just so many good memories in this old place. I've never felt, well, *safer*—anywhere—than I have, here in this house."

"Barbara," Richard said in the tone he took when he thought she was getting a bit hysterical.

"Well, it's true. And I know you've sensed it too." She looked at the ceiling as though she could see beyond it, into the attic. "I heard the music again last night."

"Honey, we've lived here for fifteen years, and for fifteen years you've been hearing things up there. Look. It's our last night in this wonderful house, so let's not spoil it; Okay? You wouldn't want to think back on tonight and regret it, would you? We've got a big day tomorrow. Put in your earplugs and try to get some sleep."

He rolled over, away from her, and turned off the light. Barbara held still for a minute, listening, straining to hear; the house was silent. She sighed, put in her earplugs, and turned toward him, oblivious to the faint strains of "Mood Indigo" which just then began to filter down from the attic.

The next day was bright and sunny and Barbara and Richard Tucker were frantic. They ran here and there, piling the last things in unmarked boxes—rolls of toilet paper, Deena's underpants, Unguentine, Janitor in a Drum, semolina—while the children were playing upstairs. Deena had put all her dolls in her red wagon and was about to pull the whole thing careening down the stairs when Scott, her ten-year-old brother, grabbed her favorite and held it hostage.

"Let's play Marie Antoinette," he said, a favorite game of his ever since he'd read *The Children's Illustrated History of the French Revolution* in fourth grade.

Deena began to scream and reach for the doll.

"Let them eat cake! Off with her head!" he yelled. He held the doll out over the bannister and with his free hand karate-chopped its head off. Deena made one last desperate attempt to grab it as the head fell spiraling toward the floor, and in the strenuousness of her effort, Deena went over the bannister herself.

She fell at the normal rate of falling objects, her head preceding the rest of her body, while her brother and she both screamed for help. And because they lived at 3847 Elmwood Drive, they got it.

Invisible hands arrested her fall, turned her right side up, and set her down on the parquet floor with unusual dignity. Scott sighed deeply and thrust his hands in his pockets. Deena looked up at the air which had saved her and murmured, "Thank you." Neither child was as surprised as he or she might have been. But then again, they'd lived in that house since they'd been born.

The moving men had loaded the last of the furniture and boxes—the Tuckers wouldn't know about the broken leg on the television or the gash in the dining room table until they arrived at Hidden Valley Estates—and the children were safe in the back seat of the station wagon when the red convertible Porsche pulled up. Rock music blared from the car's four speakers, and the man and woman sat there nodding their heads until the shivaree ended, while Richard and Barbara stood, not knowing what to do next.

Then the two opened the doors of the Porsche and stepped out.

"Hi," the man said. "You the Tuckers?" He was wearing an electric-blue polyester leisure suit; the first three buttons of his wide-lapeled red shirt were open, revealing a nest of curly black hair in which a slither of gold chains seemed to be reproducing. He walked toward them, extending a hand weighed down with rings. "I'm Tony Sepulveda," he said.

"Oh," Barbara said. "*You* bought the house."

"You got my number, sweetheart," Sepulveda said. "You dudes weren't here when that hot real estate chick showed us the joint." He pointed at the back seat of the station wagon. "What are those?" he asked. "Kids?"

"One of each," Richard said. He wasn't looking at Sepulveda, though; he was watching the woman. She wore a dress as red as the Porsche; and like it, she had her top down. Her cleavage sported a huge paste diamond, and her hair was blonde and jumbled on her head like some tortuous Escher drawing. She slunk next to Tony and leaned against him, as if for warmth. "This is my wife, Sheena," he said. "You probably recognize her."

The Tuckers looked embarrassed until Tony said, "Don't you dudes rent adult cassettes? You're looking at the star of *Thighs and Whispers*."

"There's a lawsuit pending," Sheena said proudly, in her Betty Boop voice.

"I'm her personal manager," Tony Sepulveda said. "Here's my card." He handed a rectangle of stiff white paper to Richard.

" 'Nino's for Brakes'?" Richard said.

"The handwritten side," Sepulveda said.

Barbara was looking the two of them up and down as though searching for trap doors. "Are you sure," she said, "that you'll be happy here? It's a very quiet neighborhood."

"Not for long," Tony said. "We *were* living in Bel-Air . . ."

"But then the real owners came home," Sheena said.

"It was an escrow confusion. *Anyway*. Our check cleared, right?" Tony said.

"Right," Richard said, and Tony let out an audible sigh of relief.

"Well, good luck, folks," Tony said. "Itza pleasure to meecha." He turned, wheeled Sheena, and started back toward his car.

Barbara Tucker looked quickly from her husband to the Sepulvedas, took a deep breath, and said, "There's something I think I should tell you about the house."

"Get in the car, Barbara," Richard said. "Time to go."

"They have a right to know," Barbara said.

"What?" Sheena said. "You got roaches?"

"We feel . . . I feel . . . that . . . that the house is haunted," Barbara Tucker said. "Nothing bad. It's just . . . Honey, tell them what you found out."

Richard Tucker sighed, glared at his wife, and began in a voice which betrayed utter confidence in the basic reality of reality. "It's nothing. Nothing at all. The house was built in the twenties, and the first owners were a young couple, the Chumskeys."

"Nelson and Evelyn," Barbara said.

"They lived here," Richard said, "for about thirty years until Mr. Chumskey died. Fell off a ladder getting leaves from the gutter and broke his neck. Two years later, Mrs. Chumskey died, neighbors said of a broken heart. Another couple moved in."

"And . . ." Barbara said.

"And the new owners claimed they heard noises and saw things floating."

"And . . ." Barbara said.

Richard really glared at Barbara now, but continued. "And we've heard noises," he said. "And the dog we had . . ."

"Dogs can sense psychic energy," Barbara interrupted.

". . . used to go nuts any time he went near the attic."

"Tell them about the fire," Barbara said.

Richard sighed, in deep now. "When the kids were little, we had a fire. We were all sleeping . . ."

"And would have been killed," Barbara said.

". . . but something shook me and woke me up. Is that it?" he said to Barbara. "Is that enough ghost stories for today?"

"That's it," she said proudly.

"So," Tony Sepulveda said. His eyes had narrowed to little slits. "You figure these dead Chumskeys are up in the attic. What do they eat? Insulation? Gimme a break! Do I look like I just fell off the turnip truck? You got a better offer on the house, so you're trying to pull out, right?"

"No," Richard said, waving his hands before him.

"I'm in show biz, buddy," Tony said. "That means I'm smart. You know who gave Johnny Salami his break?" He stuck his thumb in his sternum as though he wished to embed it there. "Me. That 'lewd and lascivious conduct' suit—I organized the whole thing. You can't pull one over on me."

"Just wanted to tell you," Barbara said. "Let's go, honey."

"Well thanks but no thanks," Sheena shrieked. "You just gave me the creeps."

"Come on, sugar," Sepulveda said. "Tony'll take care of you."

In the attic, everything seemed toned with sepia. Nelson Chumskey wore a dark suit with wide lapels and sat before a table set for two. He held a champagne flute in his old papery hand, and he seemed to be listening faintly to the record player which scratched away at "Someone To Watch Over Me."

Across from him sat his wife, Evelyn, in a long sum-mery lavender dress. She held a flute as well, and as the glasses came together in a little clink, Nelson said, "Happy anniversary, Beauty."

Evelyn smiled good-naturedly and cooed, "Happy anniversary, Beast."

They drank, and then Nelson stood, leaned over, and kissed his wife, and shook his head in wonder. "You still got it, Evelyn."

"You're sure it's me and not the mouthwash?" she said. Nelson Chumskey straightened the front of his jacket, brushing off imaginary lint, and then very formally walked around the table and stood beside her chair.

"Nelson, what are you doing?" Evelyn asked.

"Would you care to . . ." He made a twirling mo-tion with his index finger.

"Fingerpaint?"

"No," he said solemnly. "Dance." It seemed this was a well-rehearsed script.

"Well," she said. "You do seem nicer than the others."

The lush violins soared up the tripping steps of the melody and then took their time slowly descending. "Nice song," Nelson said.

"Mmmm."

"I think I love you," Nelson said, and kissed his wife again.

When the record was over, they sat back down and surveyed their domain—old lamps with fringed shades, creaky oak dining room chairs, and a footlocker of clothes you would now find only in costume banks and used-clothing stores. There were overstuffed armchairs upholstered in heavy green fabric; the tableware was Fiesta, the glassware Depression glass.

"It's hard to believe," Nelson Chumskey said. "It seems like yesterday. And now . . . our sixty-fifth wedding anniversary."

"Mmm," Evelyn said. "Sixty-five?"

"Sure," Nelson said. "We were married in 1922. This is 1987; that's sixty-five years. And every year it gets better."

From outside, they heard the sound of a piercing female voice raised in mock horror. "Tony Maroni! No!" Evelyn went to the attic window just as a tremendous splash and screeching laughter echoed into their domain. She saw a woman wearing a red dress which clung to the ample curves of her body like Saran Wrap, and a man wearing some shade of blue who laughed like a hyena. "Oh dear," Evelyn said. "Come look."

Nelson joined her and shook his head, even as he watched Sheena's wetly outlined rump with some interest.

"The Tuckers really left," he said. "Such lovely people. We'll miss them."

"But what do you think of these new ones?" Evelyn asked. "They look . . . a bit . . . *brassy*."

"Oh, sweetheart," Nelson said, hugging her to him. "They're just people. How bad can they be?"

A week later, the Chumskeys ventured out of their attic and made a tour of the house. The white walls had been repainted puce and mauve and salmon, and sported posters from Sheena's adult movies and cassettes. In most of them, she seemed bent backwards in the middle, in order for her heaving breasts to be front and center. The Tuckers' comfortable sofa and chairs, which had graced the living room, had been replaced by round leather bundles full of some crunchy substance which wasn't granola; they looked like partially deflated puffballs.

Evelyn found the smallest gold spoon she'd ever seen on a table in the kitchen, far smaller than her own demitasse spoons. And on the counter was something neither Nelson nor Evelyn had ever seen before, called a lava lamp.

Loud discordant music played all day and most of the night, coming from speakers in every room.

And at three o'clock every afternoon, Tony and Sheena worked for an hour in the "studio," which was also the master bedroom, now outfitted with exercise mats on the floor, black satin sheets on the bed, a videotape camera on a tripod so that Tony could record, for posterity, Sheena's gyrations, and mirrors on the ceiling and two of the walls.

Sheena attempted to sing along to recorded music; her only real talent had developed, as it were, at puberty—as far as music went, Sheena didn't know an eighth note from a trash compactor.

She was now crunching a song, the lyrics of which went:

> I want to make love to you all night
> I want to scream and kick and scratch and bite
> I want to stay hot until the morning light
> Then I'll know that everything is all right
> Everything is all right baby, all right
> Everything is all right baby, all right
> So break out the whip and handcuffs with all your might
> And tie me up, tie me up, tie me up tight

The song was called "All Right," music and lyrics by Tony ("Maroni") Sepulveda.

She was wiggling as she sang, and Tony kept exhorting her to exaggerate, a word which, in Sheena's case, was impossible to comprehend. "Sell it, baby," Tony said as he viewed her, in miniature, through the video camera's viewfinder. "Okay, now on *all right* I want a big *bump*."

Secluded in a corner of the bedroom, Evelyn and Nelson Chumskey stood watching, though, of course, neither Tony nor Sheena in the ecstacy of their artistic triumph were aware of their presence. Evelyn and Nelson, let it be noted, were less than thrilled with the new inhabitants of 3847 Elmwood Drive.

Sheena reached the big last line, shrieking the repetition as Tony yelled, "Okay, baby, now reach way down into the depths of your being. A big finish. Okay." Sheena leaped from the bed and landed on the floor in a split. Tony put down the camera and began applauding.

"That was revolting," Evelyn said.

"Did you really think it was *that* bad?" Nelson asked sheepishly.

"That was great, honey," Tony said. "Look. You made me sweat. I have tears in my eyes."

"Reeeeeally?" Sheena asked, crossing her heart with her living arms.

"Well," Tony said, backing off a bit. "One eye. I say we rehearse it one more time and then we go down to the mall, get in one of those photo booths, and shoot the album cover."

"But what about that camera?" Sheena asked.

"Just home movies, sweetie. Maybe another cassette. I been thinking about titles. How you like *Belly Button Lingo*?"

"You're so good to me, Tony," Sheena said. "Tony?"

"Yo."

"When I was singing just now I had this strange spooky feeling." She pouted suddenly, as though she'd just invented worry.

"I told you," Tony said. "Don't listen to your voice, just concentrate on the movements."

"No," Sheena said. "It wasn't my voice. I felt like people were watching. Does that sound stupid?" Sheena asked.

"Not coming from you," Tony said. "Come on, one more time."

Evelyn was embarrassed at having been sensed. "Ready, dear?" she said. "Let's go upstairs."

"What's that?" Sheena asked, cocking her head. From far away, a dog was barking ferociously.

"Oh," Tony said. "I forgot. I bought you a dog, a little present for rehearsing so hard. He's in the downstairs closet."

"Oh, Tony," Sheena said. "You locked a dog in the closet? He could eat all my clothes." Tony bolted from the room and clattered down the stairs.

She stood there, as did the Chumskeys. The sound of claws scratching wood could be heard as the dog hurtled up the steps and entered the room, nervous, high-strung, as only an untrained Doberman can be. "Oh, Tony Maroni!" Sheena shrieked. "I love him. He's so vicious. You bought him for me?"

"Well, not exactly. The pet store owner was in the back and the video security wasn't working, so . . . I named him Sheena so you wouldn't forget."

Suddenly the dog growled, lunged away from Tony, snapping madly at the air through which the Chumskeys rose, passing through the ceiling and into the attic. They shook their heads at one another. It was clear they'd have to take some kind of action; this Sheena-and-Tony couple wasn't about to settle down.

"Why are we running?" Evelyn asked. "We're dead."

"And I'd like to keep it that way," Nelson said.

Later that evening the Chumskeys were sitting on the roof, staring out over the dark neighborhood dotted here and there by the lights in second-story windows where couples were preparing for bed. Evelyn shook her head, torn between bewilderment and distaste. "What kind of people are they? Maybe it's us. Maybe we're behind the times. Maybe that's the modern way."

Nelson had clearly gotten over his interest in Sheena's shapeliness. "Did the Tuckers do those things? Did the Hunseckers?" He thought for a moment. "I don't *like* these people. They're ruining our death. Our house has an ugly feeling to it now. This is not how we wanted to spend eternity."

"Oh, eternity," Evelyn said, patting him on the back. "It's not eternity. Eventually they'll die or move out."

"Sooner rather than later," Nelson said. "We've got to get them out of here."

"But how?" Evelyn said. "They own the place."

"Well," Nelson said. "After all, we *are* ghosts. Why don't we scare the cream cheese out of these Sepulvedas?"

"Us?"

"Us!" Nelson said. "Let's be terrifying."

"I don't know, Nelson," his wife said. "Do we have it in us?"

"If I have to, I'll bring this house crashing down on their heads."

"Oh, no!" Evelyn said. "Not our house. If we do, we'll be doomed to wander in limbo and our souls will have no peace."

It was a sobering thought, interrupted by a sudden jolt of singing from the bedroom. "I want to make love to you all night," Sheena screeched.

"Let's do it," Evelyn said.

The Chumskeys waited until the noises downstairs had ceased, and then slipped through the ceiling into the Sepulvedas's bedroom. They were hunched together in the center of the bed, covered by black satin. Nelson nodded at his wife and began to make ghostly noises—a low flat *oooooo* that sounded more like air hissing from a tire than anything else.

"Ooooo?" Evelyn whispered. "This is going to send them running in terror? Let me try." Evelyn's *oooooo* was much more convincing; she let her voice wander up and down the higher scales, like an ominous wind whistling in autumn branches.

But the Sepulvedas didn't move. Evelyn nudged Nelson and whispered, "Falsetto," and the two of them together started producing some genuinely eerie noises.

Suddenly Sheena sat up, clutching the sheet to her throat. "Tony. Wake up," she hissed, and then dug into him with one of her fingernails.

"Waaa—?" he said. He rolled over and tried to cover his head with a pillow, but Sheena restrained him. "I hear noises," she said.

The Chumskeys, thrilled with their success, began *oooo*ing in earnest.

"What the hell is that?" Tony said.

"I'm scared, Tony," Sheena wailed.

"Boo!" Evelyn shouted. "Boo!" Nelson shouted.

"Toe-nee," Sheena said. "Remember what those people told us? About ghosts? Oh, Tony, I'm really scared."

"There, there," Tony said. He reached across the sheets and took her into his arms. "It's okay." He stroked her neck. "It's going to be . . ." He raised the sheet, perplexed, and looked in the direction of his groin. "Well whadda ya know? Oh, baby," he said. "Kiss me."

Sheena seemed to forget all about the *ooo*s and promptly rolled on top of Tony, nibbling his ear and neck. Tony moaned.

The Chumskeys stopped *oooo*ing and turned their backs.

Downstairs, they had another idea, interrupted by the other Sheena, the one with the brains, who was viciously biting the head off a chewed-up doll Deena had left behind. The dog promptly dropped the doll and started for the Chumskeys. "Nice doggie," Evelyn said. "Keep him occupied," Nelson said.

In the fridge he found half a roast, and with that as the bait, enticed the Doberman into a closet and slammed the door. They could hear the sounds of frenzied eating.

Then they searched for ideas. They found one: there was a videocassette of *Zombie Ghosts of Cannibal Island* and after Nelson figured out how to work the VCR, the two of them huddled together in terror and watched the hungry zombies chow down, like Sheena and the roast.

"I don't understand," Evelyn whispered. "Clark Gable kissing Vivien Leigh, *that's* a movie."

But they took their cue anyway, painted their faces green, splattered their mouths with ketchup, draped themselves with moss from the garden. The chains were a bit difficult, until Nelson remembered the dog's outside lead. Then, clanking and groaning, moaning and snarling, they re-entered the bedroom.

The Sepulvedas were still at it; now, at the foot of the bed, they looked like the pulsing throat of a black satin bullfrog.

"Oh my God," Nelson said. "Even a train stops."

"Let's get it over with, then," Evelyn said. "On three."

They counted to three and then, together, bellowed "GET OUT" in deep hideous voices. The noises on the bed stopped. "Again," Nelson coached, and the two of them together clanked the chain and screamed, "Get out! Leave this house!"

The sheet came off the Sepulvedas's terrified faces, and Sheena screamed. Tony hid behind her, using her as a shield, as the Chumskeys clomped and banged around the bedroom. The lava lamp began to shake; the overhead fixtures rattled and swung.

"Sheeeeenaaaaaa!" Tony yelled.

"What?" she said.

"Not you, stupid. Sheeenaaaa."

From downstairs they could hear the sound of wood splintering, the clatter of claws on wood as the dog bounded up the stairs toward them. The Chumskeys tried "Get out" one more time, but their hearts weren't in it; as the dog made straight for them with an open mouth, they disappeared through a wall and huddled on the other side, terrified themselves, but listening.

"Oh, Tony," Sheena wailed. "Let's get out of here. Let's just go. Tonight."

Beyond the bedroom wall, Evelyn beamed and hugged Nelson.

Then they heard the voice of Tony Sepulveda. "Wait a minute," he said. "Tony S. wasn't born yesterday."

"Of course not, honey," Sheena reassured him. "Look at how big you are."

"That wasn't no ghosts," Tony said. "It was the two sold us this place. They're out there somewhere plotting. They want the house back! You heard 'em the day we moved in. They made a bad deal and are trying to scare us out."

"But they walked through the wall," Sheena reminded him.

"No they didn't," Tony said. "Remember, I'm in the business. Special effects. I know 'em when I see 'em."

"You mean like 'Thriller'?" Sheena asked.

"You got it, baby," Tony said. "Now give me another kiss."

"They're staying," Nelson said. He was beginning to feel depressed. Nothing like being a ghost and not being able to make someone believe it.

"They're too stupid to scare," Evelyn said. She began to cry.

"Never mind, dear; never mind," Nelson said. "At least we have each other. And they won't be here forever."

"Thirty years, forty at the most," Evelyn said between sniffles.

"And we'll always have our attic, our own cozy love nest," Nelson said.

Evelyn smiled and gave her husband a big kiss on the cheek. "Oh, thank you, Beast," she said.

"You're welcome, Beauty," Nelson said.

But the next morning the Sepulvedas invaded the attic in satin pajamas. "I see one big, beautiful master suite. I see mirrors, ceiling, walls, floor. So as to take advantage of our *new transparent water bed*," Tony Sepulveda said.

"And the powder room over here?" Sheena said.

"I'm with you, baby," Tony said.

"With a heated commode?"

"His *and* hers. And I see lights, bright ones, colored ones, maybe strobes . . ."

"No!" Nelson yelled. He'd had it. Whatever it took, he knew that now was the moment to rid himself of the Sepulvedas.

"And look over here," Tony said, taking Sheena's hand and walking to the window. "You see this? Those lawns and trees and kids on bicycles? It's gone, mirrored over."

"Nooooo!" Nelson yelled. He ran as fast as he

could across the attic and with a mighty shove sent Tony Sepulveda catapulting toward the driveway below. He fell as objects fall, but a foot from the solidity of paralysis or death, he was wrenched from the fall by invisible hands and set down, none too gently, on his rump.

Sheena ran, screaming, down the stairs, through the living room, onto the driveway, screaming as though it were she who'd fallen and not Tony. She hugged him as he stood, white and panting, in his silk pajamas. Together they looked up at the attic window, then back at each other.

"Tony?" Sheena said. "Was it the Tuckers?"

"No," Tony said. "No way."

"Was it a special effect?"

Tony shook his head.

"Was it . . . ?" Tony let his head bob up and down until Sheena grabbed his hand and the two of them ran, screaming, down to the red Porsche and gunned it out of there.

Less than a month later, the Tuckers were back. There'd been little trouble in unloading the place in Hidden Valley, and from the Sepulvedas they got an extra-special deal. Now the children raced joyously in the backyard and Barbara and Richard stood by the charcoal grill watching the burgers sizzle.

"Thank you, honey," Barbara said. "It's *so* good to be home."

Richard shrugged and grinned. "What's another hour on the freeway?" he asked.

"Come on, kids," Barbara called. "Soup's on."

Above them, on the second-story balcony which overlooked the back yard, Evelyn and Nelson Chumskey sat, hugging themselves with joy.

"That wasn't nice, you know," Evelyn chided her husband. "Nothing is worth physical violence."

"Not even the loss of our attic?" Nelson asked.

"No, dear," she said. "Not even that."

But Nelson was unconvinced. "I just don't know what came over me, dear. Anyway, no one was hurt. Hungry?"

Evelyn nodded. "Just a little," she said.

Below them, Richard Tucker flipped a burger and it didn't come down. He and his wife watched a floating bun surround the burger and disappear in the direction of the roof. They laughed and hugged each other as Scott and Deena ran up, ready for supper.

Nelson sat watching his wife take a dainty bite of her burger. He shook his head. "I don't know," he said. "Is it me, or do you get better looking?"

She put down the burger and kissed him. "Sixty-five years," she said. "You look pretty good for ninety, too."

"Oh. Well," Nelson said, shrugging off the compliment. He took a deep breath. "Summer's the best, isn't it? Freshly cut grass, hickory barbecue, kids playing."

"It *is* nice, isn't it?" Evelyn said.

"It's nice to be a family again," Nelson said.

Together they leaned over and peered down at the patio, where Barbara Tucker was helping her children to a nice big lump of potato salad.

GRANDPA'S GHOST
by Steven Bauer

Based on the Universal Television series *Amazing Stories*
Created by Steven Spielberg
Adapted from the episode ''Grandpa's Ghost''
Teleplay by Michael de Guzman
Story by Timothy Hutton

EDWIN HARTLEY PUT DOWN HIS PAINTBRUSH AND stared at the canvas; he couldn't quite get her right. He sighed and looked at his watch; it was 8:30 P.M. Downstairs, his grandparents would be doing what they always did at this time of night. Having finished the dinner dishes, Helen, his grandmother, would be sitting in her armchair, waiting for something to happen, while Charlie, his grandfather, would be puttering in his study, listening to his tapes, the two of them off in different worlds, though always tied together by the love they'd shared during sixty years of marriage.

Tomorrow he and Charlie would be off to San Diego, to the zoo, and a Padres home game. It was time to go down and get the old man, who always spent the night before departure with his grandson.

When his parents had died in the car accident, Edwin had moved in with Helen and Charlie, and when he'd turned eighteen, two years before, he'd taken an apartment above them in the old building in west Los Angeles where they'd lived ever since he could remember.

He parted the curtain and looked outside; the sun was sinking fast in the west, falling into the Pacific Ocean. Its last orange wash streamed through the windows. Down below, the street and sidewalk were deserted, as though the three of them were the only ones alive in this part of the world.

Edwin walked down the two flights and knocked in his familiar pattern. He could hear the wheeze of cushions as Helen got to her feet and padded to the door, the slow methodical unlocking of three locks, and then her frail and time-worn face appeared, still lovely, wreathed in a halo of white hair. She wore one of her old housedresses, a little threadbare and faded, with a delicate pattern of small flowers. She smiled at him, as she always did, and bade him come in.

Edwin passed her and stood for a moment in the living room; the curtains on the windows overlooking the street faded from gold to thin white as the sun slipped away, and then his grandmother was beside him, touching his elbow so gently he might have imagined it.

"Where's your stuff?" she asked.

"Stuff?" Edwin said, looking down at her.

"Can't go fishing without a pole."

From behind the closed door of Charlie's study, Edwin could hear the old man singing a medley of songs to which he'd changed the words; San Francisco and New York be damned, as he'd say. "San Diego, here I come," Charlie sang. And then: "San Diego, a hell of a town/The zoo is up and the ballpark is down."

Edwin smiled and rested his arm on his grandmother's shoulders. "No, gram," he said. "We're
not going fishing. We're going to the zoo and the
ballpark."

"Oh," she said. "That's good too." She paused
and looked toward her husband's study. Then she
pushed Edwin in that direction. "Go on," she said.

Edwin walked to the door and knocked.

"I don't want to be bothered," the old man's voice
said, a bit gravelly and gruff.

"It's me, grandpa," he said.

His grandfather's voice leaped into another oc-
tave. "Well, then get in here, Edwin," Charlie said.

His grandfather was in his eighties, and even
frailer than Helen, as though he'd started shrinking
in on himself as he got older. But he was still a
powerhouse of energy. He swung around in his
swivel chair to meet Edwin as the boy entered; he was
wearing his Padres baseball cap, his old tattered
windbreaker, and a pair of black high-top Keds. A
packed overnight bag lay at his feet.

As always, Edwin was delighted and amazed by his
grandfather's study, packed on every wall, and in
piles on the floor, with memorabilia—along the top
of the sofa, the desk, and the piano, stacks of sheet
music grew brittle and yellow, the songs his grandfather had played with the bands he'd worked with.
Record albums showed their thin spines in rows and
rows, so heavy in their bulk that the shelves sagged.
Photographs of musicians, of Edwin's father as a
boy, as a teenager, of Helen—a biography in photographs—of Edwin himself, covered every available
spot on the walls.

Charlie grinned at him. "Great place, San Diego,"
the old man said. "I want to see the monkeys." He
held out his hand and Edwin helped him up. "You'll
love the monkeys, Edwin."

"I did the last time," Edwin said. He could never

be sure what year he'd find his grandfather in, or whether the past would be clear to the old man.

"Just can't see enough of those little buggers," Charlie said. "Been years since I saw them. When was the last time we went?"

"Three months ago, grandpa," Edwin said.

"Is that so?" Charlie said. "Is that so? How do I look?"

"You look good," Edwin said.

Charlie took a tottering step forward and gripped Edwin's elbow with surprising strength. "Snazzy is more like it, my boy. Always try to look snazzy, Edwin." He passed his grandson and walked to the door, one slow step at a time; his hands, when they weren't gripping something, shook slightly. "Don't forget my bag, now," he said. Edwin picked it up and waited for his grandfather to maneuver through the doorway. "Snazzy," the old man said, snapping his fingers.

In the living room, he barely looked at his wife; he headed for the door to the hallway. "Two days," Charlie said. "We'll be gone two days."

"I know that," Helen said. She motioned to Edwin, and lowered her voice. "There's something I wanted to tell you," she said.

"And we're going to a ballgame," Charlie said, still moving one slow step at a time. "Box seats, third base. Better bring your mitt, Edwin."

"It's all he's been talking about," Helen said to Edwin.

Charlie reached the door and turned back, as though he'd forgotten something. "I'm spending the night at Edwin's," he said. "Because we're leaving at the crack of dawn. She gets awful sore when I wake her up," he confided.

"I get awful sore when you *keep* me up," Helen said. Then to Edwin, as always caught between the two, she said, "Don't let him make you stay up too late. The old night owl." She shook her finger at her husband. "And make sure you take your medicine."

"I always take my medicine," he growled. "Let's go." He moved out into the hall. Edwin paused a minute with his grandmother.

"Do you need anything, grandma?" he asked.

"She never needs anything," Charlie said, sticking his head back in.

"I could use some peace," Helen said.

"Don't worry," Edwin said. "We'll just be upstairs."

"She knows where you live," Charlie said. "Edwin! Come on."

"Have a good time," Helen said. Edwin smiled at her and nodded, then bent down and gave her a quick kiss on the cheek. "Fishing!" she said, shaking her head, as though she hadn't yet gotten it straight. The door slowly closed behind him. The elevator was broken, and it was a long two flights up.

Charlie sat at the piano, playing with surprising force for someone so weak, and belting out the songs he sang with real vigor. Though his body had grown frail, his voice hadn't really diminished. Edwin sat next to him on the piano bench, singing along, but tentatively; he could never just relax and let himself go.

Charlie paused and cast Edwin a withering stare. "Come on, Edwin. Put some heart into it." He began playing again, and this time Edwin tried his best to sing with Charlie's spirit.

The old man clapped Edwin on the shoulder and laughed; the boy could tell his grandfather approved.

They retired to the couch, and his grandfather took a deep breath and stretched his legs up on an old fruit crate. The apartment, really a studio, was furnished in modern thrift shop—an old lumpy couch, a beat-up piano, a card table, and several folding chairs. "I've got a picture of her," Edwin said.

"Well," his grandfather said. "Let's see it."

"It's not finished," Edwin said.

"What do you mean?" Charlie asked. "I thought you had a picture."

"It's a painting, grandpa." He looked to the wall where he'd turned his easel around; behind it a stack of canvases leaned. On another card table his balsa-wood model of a village lay unfinished, gathering dust. He never quite seemed to finish the projects he started. "I'm just not sure how it's going to turn out."

"Let me ask you this," Charlie said. "What's her name?"

"I don't know," Edwin said.

"You don't know her name?"

"I don't need to," Edwin said. "I'll show the picture to you some other time. I stand in front of it, I stand next to it; I just can't seem to get inside it. I work on it every night. It just seems to stay the same."

"Did you do what I told you to do?" Charlie asked.

Edwin shrugged and smiled apologetically. "I go into the store just to see her, but when I get up close, my mouth won't work."

"Can't talk without your mouth," Charlie said.

"I've tried," Edwin said. "I just stutter."

"You talk fine," Charlie said.

"Around you, I do."

"Tell you what," the old man said. "I'll pretend to be you, and you be what's-her-name, Mary, we'll call her. Ready? Here goes. 'Hi, Mary, my name's Edwin. How are you?' "

"Fine," Edwin said uncomfortably.

" 'I was thinking, Mary. There's going to be a great sunset tonight. What say we take a walk on the beach and watch it together?' "

"Okay," Edwin said.

"See how easy it is?" Charlie said. "Now you be Edwin and I'll be Mary." Edwin blushed, moved to get up, but his grandfather's hand, quick as a cat, held him in place. "Come on, Edwin. Heart. Remember the heart."

"Hi, Mary," Edwin said. "My name's Edwin. How are you?"

"I'm fine, Edwin," Charlie said coyly.

"The sunset is going down," Edwin said, "and I was wondering . . ." He stopped, knowing he'd gotten it wrong. Charlie waved a hand to show him it was all right.

"I'm sorry," Edwin said. "It's hard being me. I have a much easier time pretending to be someone else."

"I was shy once," Charlie said. "I was afraid of everyone. All I could do was play the piano. I couldn't look anyone in the eye, Edwin. In those days I played everywhere—road houses, clubs, dance palaces, cocktail lounges." Relieved to be off the subject of himself, and always eager to hear Charlie's stories, even the ones he'd heard many times before, Edwin relaxed. "Between jobs," Charlie said, "I'd go fishing off the pier. Fish is good for you, Edwin. Iodine. Remember that." He patted his grandson's knee.

"I like fish," Edwin said, though in fact he hated it.

Charlie smiled, and his expression softened. Edwin could see he was traveling backwards in time. "I was playing at this club," the old man said, "right here in L.A. It's a restaurant now. Called Blackburn's. I was sitting there, playing the piano, wearing my tuxedo, looking snazzy as hell—always look snazzy, Edwin—when Johnny Ray says, 'Get up here, Charlie, and sing these people a song.' It was the first time I got the spot, a Friday night, or a Saturday, doesn't matter. Remember the fish, Edwin.''

"I will," Edwin said.

"Where was I?" Charlie said. "Oh, yeah. I was singing when I realized someone was singing with me. I looked around and saw this beauty at the table right in front of me and we locked eyes and kept singing together. When I was done, I introduced myself and we got married.''

This was the punch line Edwin had been waiting for, and he joined his grandfather in wild laughter.

"I asserted myself, Edwin. See what happens when you take a chance? Your grandmother made me a cake once, shaped like a fish, with musical notes on it. A chocolate cake. She's a wonderful woman, Edwin. I can't tell you how much I love her.''

"I know, grandpa," Edwin said.

"Listen to this," Charlie said. He began singing, *a capella,* a few lines from a haunting blues ballad Billie Holliday had made famous.

He stopped singing. "It's our song, Edwin. Haven't sung it to her in a long time.''

"That's a nice story," Edwin said.

"It's a great story. When we get back, I'm going to sing her our song.'' He smiled and stared up at the ceiling. "Know what, boy?'' he finally said. "Your old grandpa's mighty tired. Think I'll just lie down here.'' He pulled his legs off the orange crate and arranged them on the sofa. Edwin got a blanket and covered the old man.

"Good night, grandpa," he said.

"It sure was," the old man said. "It sure was.''

By the pale light of early morning, Edwin rose and made coffee. He poured his grandfather a glass of orange juice, toasted two slices of bread, and set it all on the rickety card table. Then he walked to the couch and shook his grandfather's shoulder. "Grandpa, breakfast," he said. "We've got to get going."

Charlie didn't respond. Edwin shook him again, and then again harder. Finally it occurred to him that his grandfather wasn't sleeping. He put his ear down to his grandfather's mouth, and the old man wasn't breathing. A pain blossomed in his chest, right where his lungs should have been. The sound of his grandfather's voice from the night before seemed to fill the room.

He took a walk; he found no one on the streets. At eight o'clock he let himself into his grandparents' apartment with Charlie's key. Helen was dancing in the living room, holding an imaginary partner, singing softly to herself. When she heard Edwin's footsteps, she whirled around, shocked out of her fantasy. "You haven't left yet," she said, her voice uncertain.

"The thing is," Edwin said, "you see what happened was, when I fixed him his breakfast . . ."

"You'd better be leaving soon," Helen said.

". . . and I went to wake him up, he was dead, grandma."

"Don't say such things," Helen said.

"He went to sleep," Edwin said. "He wouldn't wake up. He took his medicine. I tried to take care of him."

"Don't worry about me," Helen said, sinking into her favorite chair. "I'm fine. I have everything I need. You just take Charlie to the zoo, and enjoy yourselves."

"Listen to me, grandma, please," Edwin said.

"He so looks forward to these trips," she said. Edwin stared at his grandmother, could see she was incapable of understanding. She rose from the chair and resumed dancing. He stood for a minute watching her, and then he left.

He was the only one at the funeral service, except for the funeral director. When the short graveside service was over, he took a handful of dirt and crumbled it over Charlie's casket. Then he took Charlie's Padres cap and placed it squarely on his head.

Two days was a long time without her Charlie, and Helen spent much of the time in his study where everything reminded her of him. She touched his photograph with gentle fingers; she sifted through the stacks of sheet music, looking for songs he'd been especially fond of. When she got tired of that, she washed and ironed all his shirts. She was at the ironing board when the door opened and he came in. "Charlie!" she said. "Well, Charlie!" She rushed to him and gave him a big hug. "You're here."

"Of course I'm here," he said. "Where did you think I'd be?"

"Well, how was your trip?"

"San Diego!" he said. "Bumper to bumper traffic, and Edwin's car overheats. They don't make 'em like they used to. They don't make anything like they used to, except the monkeys."

"Did you have a good time?" she asked.

"Edwin doesn't know how to enjoy himself. You should say something to him, he listens to you."

"Did you take your medicine?" she asked.

He started for his study. "I always take my medicine. Leave me be."

"I always leave you be," she said.

"I'm going to take a nap, maybe," he said. "Maybe play the piano." From behind his closed door, she heard him noodling around on the keys. "Have to get this darn thing tuned," he said. "Can't play it any more. You'd think they could make one that would stay tuned." She returned to her ironing;

the bickering was fine with her. Charlie was home.

She made him his meager dinner—canned tuna mixed with onions and mayonnaise—as he talked on the phone to Rudy, his old friend who she'd thought had died. She was delighted she'd been wrong about that. Too many people had died; she was glad Rudy wasn't one of them. "Rudy!" she heard him say through the closed door of his study. "How are you? We had a great trip. Of course we went to the ballgame. Saw the darndest double play. Second baseman dropped a fly ball and threw the runner out at first. Then the first baseman threw the runner out at second. Top of the eighth. Tie game. Padres won." She heard him hang up the phone as she put the plates of tuna on the TV tables in the living room, then the door of his study opening.

He looked down at the tuna with disdain. "I can't stand this stuff," he said. "We're going out for dinner. Blackburn's."

Helen looked at him, startled. "Where we met?"

"And I won't hear a word against it."

"Blackburn's," she said. "What should I wear?" She bustled into the bedroom and started looking through her old dresses.

Though they seemed to be the only ones at the restaurant that evening, Helen was having a wonderful time. Charlie kept pouring more and more wine into her glass, saying, "You better drink up. You're not holding your end."

"Charles Hartley," she said, smiling. "Are you trying to get me looped?"

"You better believe I am. Besides, it's good for you."

"Cleans out the cobwebs, huh?" she said.

"At our age, it'll take a helluva lot more than a glass of wine," Charlie said. He raised his glass and toasted her. "Bottoms up," he said. He took a swallow, and Helen took a sip. The minute she returned her glass to the table, he refilled it. She slapped his hand playfully.

"Behave yourself!" she said. "I'll pass out."

"Well, if you do," he said. "I'll just swoop you up in my arms and carry you home." They both thought about that for a moment; then Helen burst out laughing. "Well," he said, "on second thought . . ." He noticed the bottle was empty and held it high. "Waiter!" he called.

"Charlie," Helen said.

"Just kidding," he said.

"Charlie, I have something to tell you, something I've never told you before."

"What?" he said. He leaned forward. His eyes were bright in the candle's glow.

"Your tie," she said. "I hate it."

"My tie?" He sat back in his chair. "I've been wearing this tie for a quarter of a century."

"I know," she said.

"Why didn't you say something before?"

"You never got me looped before. I almost said something once, back in the sixties."

"I didn't know that," Charlie said. Helen nodded. "Well, then," he said, ripping off his tie and throwing it over his shoulder. "Boy!" he said. "Damn! Is this a great time or what?"

"It's a great time, Charlie. Reminds me of that night in Hartford. Remember that?"

"Yeah, sure I do," he said. "Hey, remember that cake you made me that one birthday? Remember that?"

"The fish," she said. "That was silly . . ."

"It was chocolate," he said and smiled at her. "Every time I go off to San Diego with Edwin, I think you should be coming with me."

Across from him, radiant in the candlelight, and

never happier, she felt like a girl again, flirting with the most handsome man in the world. "You never said so before," she said.

"I'm telling you now," he said.

"Well," Helen said. "If you insist."

"Both of us do," he said. "Edwin and I."

"Maybe we could double-date, with that girl he likes. We must get him to talk to her," she said.

"If she's the right one," Charlie said, "he'll find a way. I did. With you." He paused and looked off into the darkness. "I know living with me hasn't always been easy . . ."

She felt the need to interrupt him. "Charlie," she said.

"No," he said. "I know. I know. But there's something I need to tell *you* now that you confessed to hating my tie. For sixty years, you've been my best girl. My beauty."

She couldn't have spoken if she'd had to. Choked with emotion, she took his hand and kissed it, rubbed it against her cheek. "Helen," he said. "Will you be mine? Always?" He leaned toward her and kissed her lips.

"Would you sing it for me, Charlie? Would you sing it again?"

He stood, held out his hand, and she took it, and moved with him across the empty restaurant. "As I remember," he said, "the bandstand was set in that corner." He pulled out a chair at an empty table and said, "Sit here." And then, using a glass stuffed with a napkin as a microphone, he sang to her the old Billie Holliday song that meant so much to both of them.

As he had the night they met, Helen saw him look at her, noticing the girl barely out of her teens who'd already fallen for the band's new singer. He came toward her, floating as in a dream, and took her in his arms and began to dance with her.

• • •

Before Edwin had even finished his customary three knocks, she answered the door; she held a mug of tea and was absolutely flush with excitement. "Good morning, grandma," he said.

"It's a great morning, Edwin. It's very very good. It's the best morning I can remember in a long time." She led him into the kitchen, away from Charlie's study door, and she talked in hushed vibrant tones. "Charlie took me out last night," she said. "He did. To the place where we first met. It was wonderful. We had fillet of sole, just broiled, the way Charlie likes it, and we drank too much, and talked, and talked. And we danced, Edwin, oh how we danced. We closed the joint. They had to throw us out. You should have heard us singing. We sang all night. It was . . . it was like a dream, a fantastic dream. We were young again. For a moment, it was the night we met."

Edwin nodded, delighted everything had gone off so well; she hadn't suspected a thing. "And Charlie wants to take me to San Diego," she said, "the next time you go."

"Where is grandpa?" he asked.

"In his study," she said. "Leave him be."

"I was going to make you some breakfast," he said.

"No, no," she said. "We'll be fine. You go find something to do."

"I'll be upstairs if you need anything," he said.

"Why don't you go talk to that girl of yours," she said. "The one you like so much."

"Maybe I will," Edwin said, believing it for the first time. After having so successfully convinced his grandmother, he believed he could do just about anything.

He rushed upstairs and put on the disguise again,

let himself out the window, down the fire escape, and into Charlie's study. He knew it wouldn't be much longer. "Helen?" he called. "I want my breakfast." He opened the door and walked slowly out into the living room. Helen was asleep in her chair, her breakfast tray before her. "I feel like taking a walk today. Let's go to the boardwalk. We haven't done that in a while." He moved closer to her; she had a smile on her face.

"Helen?" he said. "Can you hear me? I'll have my breakfast and then we'll go." He shuffled toward the kitchen, then turned and walked over to her chair. Even from where he stood, he could see she was dead. He looked at her for another moment, then bent over and gently kissed her.

He moved back to the study, found the tape he wanted, the tape of Charlie singing the Billie Holliday song he and Helen had loved so much. He put it in the machine, punched the button, listened to the sweet, sad music.

He'd done what his grandfather hadn't been able to do, to sing their song once more, to let Helen know how much he loved her. It was odd how people waited too long to say the things that were in their hearts, as if they had all the time in the world. Edwin resolved to talk to whatever-her-name-was. He'd wasted enough of his life. To the sounds of his grandfather singing, Edwin began to remove the disguise.

MUMMY DADDY
by Steven Bauer

Based on the Universal Television series *Amazing Stories*
Created by Steven Spielberg
Adapted from the episode ''Mummy Daddy''
Teleplay by Earl Pomerantz
Story by Steven Spielberg

THEY WERE ON LOCATION NEAR THE OKEFENOKEE Swamp in southwestern Georgia and they were shooting the mob scene; the angry townsfolk, all in late nineteenth-century garb, brandishing torches and shotguns, were in hot pursuit of the mummy which had been terrorizing the community. Led by the mayor, played by leading man Clive Rutledge, they were about to enter the swamp itself. The cameras were rolling.

Harold had answered his makeup call at 8:30 A.M. and now, almost ten hours later, he still looked like some monstrous walking piece of papier mâché; his arms and splinted legs, his torso and head were wrapped with layer upon layer of bandages. It was worse than trying to walk in a full body cast, and with the temperature in the nineties even as daylight waned, and humidity at seventy-eight percent, he was sweltering.

Perhaps worst of all, he couldn't talk; the bandages held his chin in place as though his jaw were wired, and the best he could do was grunt and whine as he tried to make himself understood. "I need water" sounded like "Ahhn waa" and though everyone tried to be as nice as they could, there were no mummy translators with the crew, and Harold was resigned to a kind of charade in which he could barely move his arms. He was a prisoner of his own costume.

At the moment he was crouched in the muck of the swamp, invisible to the cameras behind some fake plastic rushes, and all he had to do was stand up on cue and lumber forward, waving his arms and groaning horribly. But Rutledge was phobic about snakes and alligators, and it had taken all day to induce him to set foot in the water.

Now, like a craven moron, he daintily dangled his foot above the oil-slicked surface while around him the bit players waved their kerosene-soaked torches and roared in rage.

"Get in there, Rutledge!" the director screamed, and Rutledge collapsed forward as the crowd swarmed around him. Harold's back was aching. In real fury, he stood and screamed and waved his arms.

"Cut!" the director yelled. "Wrap it. That's a take. We'll break for dinner. I want everyone back on the set in an hour and a half; that's ninety minutes, ladies and gentlemen."

That was it? He'd been wrapped for ten hours for a sixty-second shot? He lumbered out of the water, covered with slime and muck, and made for the director as though to strangle him. He was getting out of these rags.

One of the bit players grabbed his elbow and said,

"Hot in there?" It was the sort of joke he'd been getting all week. "Want to join us?" the guy continued. "We're running over to that joint on the highway; you know, that gourmet place that serves rattlesnake with fangs on the side."

"Hfff," Harold said, meaning *have fun*, and the guy nodded as though he understood. "When they let you out of there, come on over," he said. "It's the place with the sign—'Good Eats, Live Bait'."

Harold headed for the makeup table, but was interrupted by Lon Lensley, the director. "Harold," Lon said, looking deep into Harold's eye holes, "you in there?" Another comic. Harold raised his arms threateningly. "Look, old buddy," Lon said, leading him toward Harold's trailer. "It'd take a good half hour to get you out of that and another forty-five to get you back in." He paused to see how Harold was reacting. "And since you're the first shot after dinner, what do you say we leave it on?" Harold stiffened under the bandages and then slumped; he knew a losing battle when he saw one. "Attaboy," Lon said. "How about a soda?"

With his splinted legs it was hard to mount the three steps into the stuffy trailer, and even harder to sit down. The bandages cut into his abdomen and made breathing difficult. Lon hustled off to the minifridge and returned with two bottles of Orange Nehi. "You know," Lon said, "confidentially, I can't help thinking we're doing something special here. Either that or a real piece of junk, it's hard to tell." He slipped a straw in the Nehi and gave it to Harold, who held it in his bandaged paws and greedily sucked on the straw. Lon looked distractedly past him to the wall where Harold had put pictures of his wife, and a picture of him in his mummy costume arm in arm with her. She looked very pregnant.

"When's she due?" Lon asked.

Harold held up his hand but had no fingers available. Like Trigger, he stamped twice.

"Two . . . ?" Lon said.

With real difficulty, Harold maneuvered his hand and stroked his face. "Uh, charades, right? Sounds like bandages, face, cheeks." Harold nodded vigorously. "Cheeks, weeks! Two weeks!" Harold touched the place his nose would have been if he'd had a nose.

"Well, it's nice she came down to visit," Lon said. "We're a long way from New York." Didn't Harold know it? He shook his head up and down. "It helps being down here, believe me," Lon went on. "The swamp, the people, the food—everything's weird. That rubs off on the picture." He took a long swallow of his soda. "Besides," he said. "This is where it really happened."

Harold cocked his head and stared at Lon. "You didn't know that, did you? Nobody does. That's why we're being so secretive. Legend has it that years ago, around the turn of the century, a traveling carnival had this real mummy. An evil Egyptian king named Ra Amin Ka; they used to charge a nickel a look, big money in those days. Anyway, one night they're putting on their show, and the thing comes to life. The few who made it out alive swore to their dying day that it still roams this swamp."

Harold looked at Lon and squinted his eyes. Then he held his sides and pantomimed laughter. What a load of crap. What a con this Lensley was. "Yeah," Lon said, and shrugged. "Well, it sells tickets."

There was a sudden knocking on the trailer door, and the assistant director burst in, looking worried.

"Harold, we just got a call. Your wife went into early labor. They took her to the hospital in Gridley."

Before he even knew what he was doing, Harold

was on his feet, lumbering past Lensley, down the steps, pushing the assistant director away, moving as fast as he could toward the Rent-a-Wreck which stood beside the trailer. "Harold," Lensley yelled behind him. "Change first."

But Harold had no intention of letting the makeup man unwind him. He was in the driver's seat before the other two men could stop him. "Harold, wait," Lensley yelled. "We'll get a driver for you." The engine roared, Harold stepped on the gas, and the Rent-a-Wreck sped out of there.

He wasn't sure where Gridley was; like everyone connected with the picture, he'd stayed away from town on Lensley's orders. Now he careened along a country road hoping for a road sign. He checked his wrist for the time, but instead of his watch, he saw dirty bandages. Then the engine began making ominous sputtering noises and the car began to slow down. Harold panted in anger and looked at the gas gauge; the needle was on E.

Up ahead he saw a small country gas station, just a pump shining under one light, in front of a small tacky white house. He grinned hugely under his bandages, thrilled with his luck.

Ezra Bunk sat in front of his TV set, watching the Friday night movie; he'd seen it before, an old black-and-white horror flick called *The Mummy's Kiss*. He heard the car pull into the pump, but was glued to the screen—if he remembered right, the guy with the turban was about to open the coffin and the mummy would come to life. "Be with you in a minute," he called. The violins started really sawing away, a sure sign of horror. From behind him he heard the steady ping of the pump. Must be one of the boys, he thought, hepping hisself.

He was right; with a flourish, the turbaned man

threw open the coffin which stood on end, and inside was the mummy, wrapped all in dirty bandages, real nasty. Suddenly, from its eye holes, light began to shine, and then it lurched forward and began to walk.

Behind him he heard a banging on the door. "Okay, okay," he yelled and regretfully pulled himself from the set. He shuffled out to get the money, and through the glass saw something he didn't believe. The mummy from the movie was standing at the door. He looked back at the TV, and the mummy stalked forward through the crowd, swinging its bandaged arms. He looked back at the door, and the mummy raised its bandaged arm. On the screen, a woman began shrieking in horror and Ezra Bunk screamed too. He ran to the door and bolted it, let the venetian blinds fly down. Then he rushed to the TV set and wrenched the plug from the wall. The screen shrunk to a pinpoint of light, then went totally blank. The banging had stopped.

He crept to the door and cautiously lifted the blind. There was nothing outside but the pump and the full moon. Ezra Bunk shook his head in wonder, then walked into the kitchenette to get a beer.

The screaming had put Harold off, given him an excuse. He'd had no money to pay for the gas, but thought at least he'd explain. But when the old man began shrieking, Harold turned and lurched back to the car, gunned it off down the road. His only regret was that he hadn't gotten directions.

Ahead, in the light of the moon, he could see the road branched and a road sign quivered in the gusting wind. GRIDLEY 6 MILES it said, and Harold grunted in relief. But as he watched, the wind swung the sign completely around so it pointed in the opposite direction; it swung again, pointing as it had when he'd first seen it. He was shaking his head in disbelief when he saw the approaching headlights.

Willie Joe Baffle was heading for a bite of rattler when he saw the car stopped at the crossroads. He put on his brakes and swore under his breath; then he realized the figure flailing its arms in the middle of the road was a mummy.

"Yaaaa!" he yelled. His foot tried to go through the floorboards, but the dirt of the country road offered little resistance. The pickup's wheels locked and Willie Joe went into a skid. In the glare of his brights, he saw the mummy glow white and horrid as he slid inexorably sideways and slammed broadside into the car. The mummy started toward him, waving its arms. He knew what mummies did to people, or thought he knew, and he yelled as he reached behind him for the loaded shotgun he kept on the gunrack for moments just like this.

He grabbed the trigger by mistake and the gun went off, blowing a hole through the side of his truck. The mummy stopped short, obviously impressed by Willie Joe's firepower, and then stumped off into the woods. "Living Jesus," Willie Joe Baffle said. "It was Ra Amin Ka."

Jubal Plinkett was out a-courtin', doing as he knew a grown man should. He swung on the porch swing with Ruta Mae Wombat, nervous as a weathervane in a windstorm. Ruta Mae wore some scent she said was called "Passion Flower" and her painted lips looked black in the full moon's light.

"You know, Jubal," Ruta Mae said. "It's a lot of fellas come courtin' me, but they was mosely just boys if you know what I mean." She moved closer and Jubal swallowed hard. "I'm a growed wooman," Ruta Mae said. "I got a wooman's desires, a wooman's needs." She took his shotgun from his lap and leaned it against the porch railing. "And a wooman needs a man, Jubal, a real man."

"I'm a real man," Jubal Plinkett said.

"Well, prove it," Ruta Mae said. Her fingers began unbuttoning his workshirt and scratching his chest, and then her lips were on his like a suction cup. From deep in her throat, she began growling.

Jubal kissed her back; something was happening, and it felt okay. He closed his eyes, then opened them; when he saw the mummy take the bicycle leaning against the front gate he fainted dead away.

The next thing he knew, Ruta Mae Wombat was slapping his cheeks and saying, "Oh Jubal, oh Jubal, was it good for you?"

The news traveled fast, and by 9:30, the concerned citizens of Gridley were gathered in the grange hall. The mayor, Winkie Nims, was trying to gavel the crowd to order, but everyone wanted to have his say at once.

"It was just horrible," Jubal Plinkett said. "The creature was all bandaged up and fire was shooting out of its eyes."

"Bullpucky," Ezra Bunk said. "Thing came right outta my TV and went straight to drinking unleaded."

"It weren't none of that there," Willie Joe Baffle said. "I knows what I knows, and that was Ra Amin Ka, hisself, I swear to Jesus."

Winkie Nims banged his gavel once more and the crowd quieted. "Now we *have* got trouble here," he said. "Even before the thing was spotted you could feel something bad was in the air. My hens stopped laying. Hank there's milk cow went dry."

"And I've taken to the bottle," Willie Joe said, brandishing the beer he was guzzling.

"Willie Joe, you always drank," Ezra Bunk said.

"Sure," Willie said. "But from cans."

"Okay, okay," Winkie Nims said. "Let's us quiet down. We know something's out there. The question is, what do we do about it?"

Everyone turned to Wendell Fink, the oldest man in Gridley, a fount of knowledge and wisdom if ever there was one. "You know," Fink said, "back in twenty-six I was living over at Possum Hollow. That summer we was paid a visit by the Swamp Hoogie. Freaked the whole town, he did, wreaked havoc on man, beast, and crops. And the question rose: 'What are we gonna do about it?' So we held this big meeting and finally we came up with an answer." He stopped for a moment and chewed his gums speculatively. "One night when it was real dark," Fink said, "we all packed up and moved away. Worked like a charm."

"Well I ain't movin' no place," Willie Joe said. "I say we grab us our shotguns and our hunting dogs, track the thing down, and blow it to kingdom come."

That brought the crowd to its feet, yelling agreement.

But Emma Primley stalked to the front of the room and held up her hands. She was the town librarian and she guarded the Erskine Caldwell and Grace Metalious novels with aplomb; she also had a soft spot in her heart for stray cats and wounded birds. "Wait a minute! Please!" she said. Since she was one of the only people in Gridley who could read, they listened to her.

"I can't believe what I'm hearing," she said. "We don't know what this thing is. Maybe it's harmless. Maybe it's lost. Maybe it's more scared of us than we are of it. Before you rush off and do something,"— she stood tall and her voice rang out—"something

you may regret for the rest of your lives, just stop a
moment and think!''

Everyone stopped for a moment and thought.
Then, ''Let's get him!'' Willie Joe yelled, and the
crowd followed him out the grange hall door,
screaming for blood.

Harold was having a difficult time with the bicycle.
He'd worked the splints out of the bandages, but still
his legs didn't bend very well at the knee and he was
forced to ride standing up, tipping from side to side
as he wobbled down the road.

Almost before he knew it, the road ended
abruptly, and the bike with him on it had toppled
over; he lay among rocks and briars and something
hard and metallic. It was a sign, riddled with bullet
holes and rust, and it said DEAD END.

''Shi—'' Harold said and scrambled to his feet. He
whirled around, peering through his eye holes to see
what he could see. His breath was harsh and loud,
but he also heard something else, something that
sounded like the baying of dogs. In the distance he
saw what looked like flickering torches, and the
torches and dogs were headed toward him.

He slogged along away from the posse, moving as
fast as his bandaged legs could carry him. And then
he saw a cabin way off in the woods, totally isolated.
Except for the dim glow of candlelight in a window,
the place was almost invisible. He tried to quiet the
hammering in his chest, and crept forward as quietly
as he could.

Harold hunched below the window, and then
slowly raised his face and stared in. An old man sat
before a peat fire, quiet and peaceful. Harold
couldn't see a gun.

Though his experiences thus far had led him to expect very little of the good-hearted people of Gridley,

he went to the door; even as he stood there his wife was in labor. He had to get to her. He took his life in his bandaged hands and raised one to knock. But before he could, the door swung open, and he was face to face with the old man.

He had straight white hair and a grizzled beard and his eyes were the milky white of sloughed snakeskin. Harold clasped his hands together as best he could and grunted beseechingly.

"Are you lost?" the old man said in a voice cracked from disuse.

"Ugh hum," Harold said, nodding his head.

"Come in, come in," the man said. "I am a friend." Harold followed the man inside.

The place was a curious jumble. Herbs and cattails hung from the rafters; mixed among the junk, Harold saw a few items of real value—a silver box, a bowl of old Chinese coins. Everything was shrouded in cobwebs and dust.

"You must be full of the night's chill," the man said. "Let me take your wrap."

Harold stepped back and said, "Nooo, daa oh kay."

"Very well," the man said. "Then some hot tea to warm your bones." He moved to a small gas stove and fumbled around for the kettle, turned on the burner, and held his palms over the stove until he'd located the flames. It suddenly occurred to Harold that the old man was blind. "Now it will be just a moment," he said, and reaching out he grabbed Harold's arm.

His head jerked to the side in bewilderment as he felt the bandages under his fingers. He patted Harold's arm, up past the elbow, the shoulder, until he touched the head. He pulled back his hands as though he'd been stung, and stumbled backwards a few steps. "Ra Amin Ka?" he said. "Ra Amin Ka?"

Then he turned and tottered off into the darkness, as if looking for something. Frightened, Harold followed, and watched in amazement as the man stopped before what he'd been trying to find. "You should be in here," the man said. "You should be . . ."

It was a sarcophagus, and the old man opened it. Inside was a mummy, a real one, and Harold watched in horror as its eyes blinked suddenly open, red as fire. "You *are* in there," the old man said. "I thought you was . . ."

But Harold didn't wait to hear the rest. He was already running.

Willie Joe Baffle shook his head in disgust; his poor pickup was in need of some body work. The rest of the mob examined the mummy's vehicle by torchlight. They mumbled and grumbled, kicking at the dirt; some of them were yawning. The mummy hunt had turned out to be more work than fun.

"Looks like it ain't our mummy," Ezra Bunk said. "Outta state plates."

"Let's go," Willie said. "We's wasting precious time. That thing could be eating innocent women and children. We gotta keep movin'."

Jubal Plinkett sauntered up to Willie, jittery and slump-shouldered. "Me and the boys been thinkin'," he said, "what we's going to do with this here mummy iffen we catch him."

"Yeah?" Willie Joe said.

"And we decided to think some more at home," Jubal said, turning to go.

Willie grabbed him by the shirt collar. "Ain't nobody running out," he said.

"It ain't that we's scared," Jubal whined. "It's just that we's puzzled. Mummy's special kind of critter, already been killed oncet."

"We drive a stake through his heart, okay?" Willie said. "Now come on."

"That ain't how you kill no mummy," Ezra said. "That's how you kill Dracula."

Willie Joe gave Ezra a withering stare, then released Jubal. "Fire, then," he said. "They hate fire."

"Huh uh," Ezra Bunk said. "Frankenstein hates fire."

Willie Joe looked worried, and stared off after his prize dog Spot who was lifting his leg on Willie's front tire. "Silver bullet," Willie said.

"Werewolf," Ezra said.

"Werewolf," Jubal said, shaking his miserable head.

"Okay," Willie Joe said. "Maybe I ain't sure how to kill a mummy."

"Let's go, boys," Jubal Plinkett said.

Willie grabbed his neck before he could move. "But that," he said, "just gives me a chance to do something I likes even better than killing. Experimenting."

Jubal was having trouble breathing. "I wouldn't miss that for the world," he gasped.

Harold's breath heaved in his chest; he'd been running for he didn't know how long, thrashing around in the woods, looking for a way out. He feared he'd been going in circles. Tree branches snagged his bandages which now fluttered around him like torn flags. He had paused for a gulp of air, leaning against a tree for support, when he felt the paw on his shoulder.

Harold screamed, almost leaping from the bandages, as he came face to face with Ra Amin Ka. The mummy was taller than he was by a good two feet, with a torso like a tree trunk, and those two burning eyes. It swung its arms the size of culvert piping and growled, and Harold was off again.

He wasn't sure, but he thought he was outdistancing the thing; he could hear it crashing in the underbrush behind him. Or was that his own noise, his own frenzied scrambling? Without warning, he stumbled into an ancient cemetery, its headstones crumbling like rotten broken teeth. A newly dug grave yawned at his feet, waiting for a corpse. He spun around but the real mummy was nowhere to be seen.

He took a deep breath and bent over, resting his bandaged hands on his knees. When he looked up, he thought he saw lights glimmering in the distance, electric lights, not the flicker of torches. Was it Gridley? Had he found his wife?

He heard a growl and turned to his right to find Ra Amin Ka wambling toward him, groping for him. It was do or die.

Harold quickly adopted a karate pose and chopped at the air with his bandaged hands. "Yaa!" he yelled as he thrust his foot at the mummy in an awkward approximation of a karate kick. "Kuu foo!" he yelled.

The mummy paused, bewildered by this strange behavior, then kept on coming. When he was within striking distance, Harold screamed "Tae tha!" and kicked again, landing his ragged foot directly in the mummy's dusty chest.

Ra Amin Ka didn't budge; like the jaws of a trap, his huge paws fastened on Harold's ankle, and he lifted Harold completely off the ground.

Dangling upside down, Harold swung, totally at the whim of the merciless mummy who decided, suddenly, to bounce Harold on the ground. "Yaaa!" Harold screamed as he pounded dirt with his head.

He did the only thing he could think of; as he bounced he reached behind him and grappled with the mummy's bandages, finding loose ends and tying them together like shoelaces. Ra Amin Ka grunted in surprise, bumbled backwards, and released Harold as he tottered and fell into the open grave.

Harold landed on his head and then his back, and lay there grunting, the wind knocked out of him. He thought he heard what sounded like a motorcycle backfiring, and then he flopped over onto his belly and scrambled off to hide behind one of the few tombstones still standing.

Two figures emerged from the darkness, an older man wearing a black beret, and a younger slack-jawed man with a shovel and a huge flashlight.

"It's a art," the old man said, "grave robbing. Takes years of sperience to know which stiffs got the gold, which grave's warm and which grave's cold."

The slack-jawed man flicked on the flashlight and pointed it at the ground. "How about that one?" he said.

The old man's hand snaked out and knocked the flashlight from the younger one's grasp. It hit the ground with a thud and rolled into the open grave. "What are you, crazy?" the old man hissed. He cuffed the younger one's ear. "Why don't you send up a flare, tell the whole country we're here?" He wiped his mouth with the back of his hand. "Now get ready for lesson number two."

Harold watched as a beam of light suddenly illuminated the faces of the two men. A bandaged hand holding the flashlight stuck up out of the grave. The older man reached over and took it. "Why, thank you," he said.

Both men screamed in terror and staggered backwards as Ra Amin Ka emerged from the open pit. They were gone, hooting through the underbrush, before the mummy managed to throw itself heavily back on firm ground.

Harold broke for the cemetery gate, and found the graverobbers' motorcycle just where they'd left it. The key was in the ignition, and Harold flipped it on, gave the starter a kick, and in a backfire of blue exhaust, left the cemetery and mummy behind.

Lon Lensley was flipping the pages of the script, trying to ignore Clive Rutledge. "Cottonmouths?" he said. "Haven't seen one. No coral snakes either. Listen, we've got to get rolling." He pushed Rutledge aside and yelled to his assistant. "Get the Gridley Hospital on the phone and find out about Harold, will you? Jesus."

The assistant director dialed the number and waited, as Lensley hovered near. "Hello? Hello, Gridley Hospital?" he said. "Has Mrs. Abbott had her baby? What? Well, is Mrs. Abbott's husband there? Harold Abbott? What?" He covered the receiver and looked at Lensley.

"She wants," he said, "to know what Mr. Abbott looks like."

Harold followed the winding dirt path, throwing earth and gravel behind him. When he reached the road, he hesitated, looking right and left. Which way were the lights of Gridley? Which way was his wife? He shrugged, turned left, and rode right into the face of the screaming mob.

"There he is!" Willie Joe Baffle yelled.

Harold veered off the road and into the woods on the far side, into a swamp. The cycle sank fast and the engine died as Harold gunned the throttle. He stood in the muck, now to his knees, and turned in the direction of the mob. In the torchlight, their faces looked scared, uncertain. He had the feeling he'd been there before.

Then he remembered: This was the scene from the

movie! And it was time for the performance of his life.

He stood quite still, waiting for the mob to quiet. He raised his arms slowly, hunched his shoulders. From deep within his bandages he gathered his force and roared and started stumping forward, keeping his legs as stiff as he could.

The crowd didn't run. He heard the sound of rifles being readied. He saw dozens of shotgun barrels pointed at his chest. He sighed. He groaned. He lifted his hands above his head.

They sat him on a horse, or what passed for one in those parts, a swaybacked, knock-kneed hag who looked to be a hundred. They placed a noose around his neck and fastened the rope's end to a branch above him. The crowd hadn't had so much fun since the funeral of Preacher McDivott. Only Ezra Bunk looked worried.

"I'm telling you, Willie Joe. Lynching's not for mummies. Lynching's for rustlers."

"Lynching's for everybody," Willie Joe said, pushing the old man aside. "Okay, now, everybody listen up." The crowd quieted.

Willie Joe puffed himself up like a big balloon and strutted back and forth before the swayback. "Well, boys," he finally said. "We done it. We caught us old Ra Amin Ka hisself."

The crowd went wild; they screamed and stamped and waved clenched fists in the air. Harold tried to yell, to tell them he wasn't a mummy but Harold Abbott whose wife was having a baby.

"Look at him now," Willie Joe said disdainfully. "That'll teach him to mess with clean decent country folk. Well, boys, what do you say?"

"Hang him!" the mob screamed, waving its arms.

Emma Primley, using her arms as a plough, wig-

gled her way to the front of the mob. "Wait a minute! Please!" she said.

"Ahhh, your mother," someone said.

"Not again," someone else said.

Emma's cheeks were burning with indignation.
"Hasn't this gone far enough?" she asked. "I mean,
is this the kind of people we are, people so eaten up
by ignorance and fear that we have to destroy something just because it's different?" She grabbed young
Slaw Fredericks, towheaded and freckle-faced, and
roughly pulled him beside her. "Is this the example
we want to set for innocent young children?"

The crowd began mumbling, kicking at the dirt.
She'd shamed them, and they looked abashed.

"Maybe there's good mummies and bad mummies," young Slaw said, looking up at Harold. "You
look like a good one."

Harold took a deep breath, one he'd thought
might be his last.

"Course," Slaw said. "You *could* be a bad one."
He turned to the mob. "I say we hang him just in
case."

The crowd roared its approval and pushed forward, shunting poor Emma aside. "Well," Willie
Joe said, winding up his underhand pitch. "Nice
knowing you." He delivered a stinging slap to the
horse's rump. "Hyah!" he yelled.

The old horse's eyes flew open, and he bolted forward. Harold felt the noose slither right up over his
head, for he had no neck at all, no place for the rope
to catch; he kicked the horse in fury.

"He's getting away!" Willie Joe yelled, and the
mob surged forward in hot pursuit as Harold hung
on for dear life, escaping once again.

He managed to free his hands which Willie Joe had
tied, but he still had a great deal of difficulty holding
on. Every hundred yards or so, the horse seemed

ready to drop over dead, but Harold kept kicking
and yelling, and the horse kept hobbling forward.

He found the road, and this time, miraculously, a
sign which read HOSPITAL 1 MILE.

He pulled the horse up in front of the hospital's
front door and in the panic of the moment managed
a western-style dismount. The crowd wasn't far behind him for the horse had been, let's face it, slow.
He rushed inside and grabbed a crutch from an elderly woman who promptly crumpled to the floor.
"Sawy," Harold said, as he thrust the end of the
crutch through the door handles just as the torch-
wielding mob splattered against the glass. They
screamed and shook their fists as Harold bolted
away, looking for help.

A doctor and a nurse walked down the hallway;
the doctor was reading a chart, and the nurse seemed
totally absorbed in the doctor. Harold tried to get
their attention, but he was understandably skittish
now. The doctor glanced up, then back at his chart.
"Nurse Pritchett," he said, "see that those bandages
get changed."

He decided to try to find his wife by himself. He
opened a number of doors, but was greeted each time
by a terrified scream. His heart was sinking fast when
he heard a flat, level voice say, "Hold it."

Harold Abbott turned to see a uniformed hospital
guard pointing a revolver at him. "Outside," the
guard growled. "You can't be dressed like that in
here."

Outside? He had to be kidding. The mob stood
glued to the door, screaming for bloodshed. Harold
tried to explain, but it was no use.

Just as he'd finally given up and started toward the
doors, a nurse wheeled a cart down the hallway, and
on the cart was his wife, holding a tiny baby.

"Harold?" she said. "Harold, is that you?"

Relief flooded him. He started toward her but the guard intervened. "You know this thing?" he asked.

"Of course," she said. "He's my husband." Harold rushed to her side, tears welling in his eyes. "It's a girl, Harold," his wife proudly said. "Eight pounds, eleven ounces. She's got your eyes." Harold grasped her hand and said "Ahh luuuyu."

"Harold," his wife said, looking at him. "Honey, what took you so long?"

Lon Lensley glanced up from his script and saw the mummy tottering toward him through the swamp. Well, maybe the night wasn't wasted. There wouldn't be too many full moons to take advantage of. "Harold," he yelled. "I thought we'd lost you, old buddy. Well, is it a boy or a girl?"

"Arrghhhggg," the mummy said.

"Right, right," Lon said. "You tell me after the shot."

It was great, everything Lensley had hoped for. He could have sworn he saw fire flash from Harold's eyes; he couldn't believe how otherworldly were the sounds which issued from Harold's mouth. The crowd responded as well, in genuine terror.

"Cut. Print. That's a wrap. Thank you, everyone." He took the mummy's arm and guided him toward the makeup table. "That was great, Harold. What a day you've had."

He stuck a big cigar in the mummy's mouth. "Congratulations," he said. "Probably feels like you've been in there for a thousand years, huh? Let's get you out of these rags."

ALAMO JOBE
by Steven Bauer

Based on the Universal Television series *Amazing Stories*
Created by Steven Spielberg
Adapted from the episode ''Alamo Jobe''
Teleplay by Joshua Brand and John Falsey
Story by Steven Spielberg

JOBE FARNUM CROUCHED BEHIND THE RUDELY BUILT stone wall as the thunder of cannons, the crackle of gunfire filled the air. One after another he loaded the rifles shoved at him and handed them back to the other Texans. His own rifle was by his side.

It was March 19, 1836, the thirteenth day of the siege. Santa Ana's men had flown the red flag of "no quarter" and against the odds, even Jobe knew there was no chance of victory. Though his compatriots were the bravest of the brave, good fighting men all, there were less than two hundred of them, and over six thousand Mexicans. It was his last day on earth.

The Alamo had served as military headquarters for the Mexicans, an important symbol of their power and authority. When a band of Texans under the leadership of colonels William Barret Travis and James Bowie captured the fort in December of 1835, it was only a matter of time before the Mexicans tried to retake it. In January, General Sam Houston received word of the impending invasion of a large Mexican army, and he ordered the Alamo surrendered.

Travis, Bowie, and the others decided to stay. Travis sent out an urgent call for aid, but only thirty-two men responded—among them Seth Farnum and his fifteen-year-old son Jobe. In the face of what seemed certain doom, Travis drew a line in the dirt with his sword, challenging the men who elected to stay and defend the fort to cross the line. All but one of them did.

"Now, boy," the man crouched by the wall yelled, but as Jobe extended the gun to him, the man stood straight up as if jerked by a wire, and toppled backwards, half of his head blown away. The Mexican who had fired the shot was running at top speed, his rifle in his hands like a club, heading for Jobe. Jobe tried to stand and run, but all strength had left him and he watched his death approach with something like peace. Then suddenly the Mexican dropped the rifle and his hands flew up in the air; he fell face-forward into the dirt, a knife stuck in the middle of his back. Jobe looked up to see Jim Bowie, so sick he could barely walk, whose knife had saved his life.

"Give Mr. Crockett a hand, Jobe," Bowie said. "I'm all right."

"Yessir, Mr. Bowie." Jobe stood and saluted; Bowie barely returned the gesture.

The boy hunched low and ran, stumbling over the fallen bodies of his comrades. As he passed an overturned wagon, a cannonball whizzed overhead. Instinctively Jobe fell to a prone position, nuzzling the dirt. He looked up in time to see a Mexican who'd broken through the walls charging toward him, toward Crockett who stood above the rubble, firing boldly. Jobe thrust out his rifle, catching the Mexican in the shin; the man howled and stumbled. "Davey!" Jobe yelled, and Crockett whirled and nailed the Mexican. But as Jobe watched, he saw Crockett rock backwards a little and look in surprise at his arm.

The boy scrambled to his feet and, keeping low, ran to Crockett's side. "Are you all right, Davey?" he asked.

Crockett nodded in the direction of a dead man on the ground. "Tear off his shirt and tie it around my arm," he said. "That's a good boy." Jobe did as he was told. "Where's Colonel Travis?" Crockett asked as Jobe tied the bandage tight around the wound.

"The Colonel's fighting over by the water supply," Jobe said.

"You're a brave boy," Crockett said.

The praise embarrassed Jobe; he was only doing what he knew was right. "No more'n you or anybody else, sir," he said.

"Maybe," Crockett said, staring off at the clouds of smoke rising above the Alamo. "How old are you, Jobe?"

"Fifteen, sir."

"You should have got out with the women and children when you had a chance, son."

"No, sir," he said firmly. "I reckon I belong here. My father died here, and I will too if that's the way it's to be."

Crockett stood and put his good arm around Jobe's shoulders. "Your daddy would be proud of you. Go see if Travis needs some help."

"But what about you?" Jobe asked.

"It'll take more'n a bullet to fell Davey Crockett,"

he said and nodded toward the water supply. "Now git."

Jobe began to run across the compound, this time without fear of getting hit; he ran upright, making a straight line for Travis, vaulting the rubble and bodies in his way. When the ground exploded before him, rocking him backwards, he staggered into a cache of powderkegs, and fell among them, hitting his head. Momentarily stunned, he rubbed his eyes; the world was spinning. He shook his head to clear his vision, and when things returned to normal, he saw the battle roaring all around him. And next to him, something like a dream.

He saw a man and a woman dressed in clothes unlike anything he'd ever seen before. The man was wearing a flimsy shirt covered with brightly colored flowers, like spider mums, like fireworks, and short pants—the kind a little boy might wear. His legs were hairless and bony and white as the smoke which hovered over his head. The woman was wearing pants which looked like leather and a bright orange shirt. But most astonishing, they seemed oblivious to the gunfire, the bodies, the battle raging around them. "Step over there, honey," the man said, motioning to the woman. "Let me get one more sequence here for the kids." He had a strange black boxlike contraption on his shoulder, and he was squinting to look through some sort of eyepiece.

"I can't stand this any more," the woman said. "I wish video had never been invented."

"This is great stuff," the man said. "I'm getting some fabulous stuff."

"Stan took Patsy to Paris for *their* twenty-fifth anniversary," the woman said, looking offended.

"Come on," the man said. "The kids'll love this."

"Fred and Janet went to Rio," the woman said.

"Come on," the man said. "Look happy."

"I'm sorry, Maury," the woman said. "I just can't get excited about the Alamo." She looked at the ground with real distaste. "It's so dusty." Without regard for the man and his contraption, the woman disappeared behind a stack of supply boxes. "Aw, honey," the man said, walking after her.

Jobe was completely befuddled. Who were these people, and how in the world couldn't they see what was happening around them? Where had the woman come from? And what were those things they were wearing? Jobe staggered to his feet and followed them, but when he turned the corner, they'd disappeared. What faced him was a dead end, a blind alley leading to a stone wall, and as he watched, an explosion sent rocks and mortar flying, and a small band of Mexicans vaulted the rubble and began running toward him. Jobe raised his rifle and fired. One Mexican fell; the others came at him. He stepped backwards, trying to reload even as he retreated, and then stumbled against something hard. He whirled around.

A woman with hair piled high on her head lounged behind a counter; across from her another woman, holding an infant securely on her hip, was examining two brightly colored rectangles of cardboard.

"Those postcards are seventy-five cents each, ma'am," the one behind the counter said. Jobe turned in shock and saw three other people he'd never seen before—a boy about his age with stiff hair, cut short on the sides and longer on top, a man in blue slacks and a short-sleeved shirt, a woman in a thin white dress. The man was holding up an undershirt with a picture of the Alamo on it.

"I don't want one of those, dad," the boy said. "I want one of the Iceman."

"They don't have George Gervin tee-shirts here," the man said.

The woman held up another one. "How about this one?" she asked. "San Antonio. Your friends can't object to that."

"Oh, all right," the boy said. The three of them walked to the woman behind the counter.

"That'll do it," he said.

"Two souvenir tee-shirts, one mug, one pendant, three postcards," the woman said, punching buttons on something on the counter. The machine whirred and clicked and bright blue numbers flashed on a little screen. "That comes to $24.95," she said. The man handed her two bills. "Out of twenty-five," she said.

"Hey, this is cool!" the boy said, holding up a small copy of a Conestoga wagon.

"Put that down," the man said.

"You all come back now," the woman behind the counter said. "Have a nice day." The family moved off. Jobe was stunned. What was happening? It was as though he'd broken through a thin wall, made of air, into another time. He followed the threesome who walked among the carnage as though it were invisible to them. "I'm going back to the hotel," the boy said, "to call Amy."

"You're doing nothing of the sort," the man said. "You'll stay right here with us."

"Mom," the boy said, petulant and whiny.

Two Mexicans were headed, rifles ready, right for the three of them. "Get down!" Jobe yelled as he fell to the dirt, rifle fire spraying the ground at the people's feet. They seemed not to notice it, just kept walking. Jobe picked up his head and stared at them.

"We didn't come all the way here for you to spend your time on the phone," the man said.

"She'll kill me if I don't call," the boy said. To their right, an explosion ignited a covered wagon, like the one the boy had held. "Get down!" Jobe yelled. "You'll be killed."

"I'm sure Amy will understand if you call a little late," the woman said.

"I think what we all need is something to eat," the man said. "I'm starving."

"Me too," the woman said.

Jobe ran toward them, yelling, "Who are you? What are you doing here?" But before he could quite reach them, another explosion rocked the ground before him, and he fell, covered with rubble and dirt.

Hands pulled him free, and he looked up into the dirt-smeared face of Colonel Travis. All around him the battle continued, but Jobe could see no sign of the people who'd been there a minute before. "Where did they go, Colonel Travis?" he said, struggling against the hands which held him down.

"Get down, Jobe," Travis said.

"Who are they?" Jobe asked. "People, those people, where did they go?"

"What the hell are you talking about, boy?" Travis said. "Now get down!" But Jobe scrambled to his feet and started darting among the rubble. He could make no sense of what was happening to him; it was like a dream, but like no other he'd ever had before. Maybe he was already dead? Maybe this was what all eternity would be like?

But then he looked squarely at a stone wall, a wall with the firm solidity of reality, and he knew where he was: A cannonball collapsed the wall and Mexican soldiers poured through, firing wildly as they ran. In terror Jobe retreated, until he hit something solid which rocked against his onslaught. It was a tall squat rectangle of metal, bright red on top with a swirl of white, in which the word COKE was emblazoned in red letters. He looked back at the gap in the wall and instead of Mexican soldiers, he saw a group of people like the ones he'd just seen. They had dark glasses on, and carried small black things on straps around their necks, which they kept holding up to their eyes as they pressed little levers and buttons.

In front of them was a woman in a uniform who said, "And after thirteen days and nights of heroic battle, this small but gallant band of freedom fighters succumbed to overwhelming odds and were wiped out to the last man. The legendary Jim Bowie, after whom the Bowie knife was named, was but one of a number of famous historical figures to give up their lives here. Davey Crockett and Colonel William Travis were two other notables."

Jobe turned and saw Davey Crockett firing his rifle, wounded, yes, but definitely alive. He spun back toward the group which had disappeared. "No!" he screamed. "It's a lie."

A hand slapped him hard across the chin, and he looked up, stunned, into Travis's face; the man had him now by the shoulders and was shaking him. "Snap out of it, Jobe," the man said. Jobe looked around him; all he could see was smoke, damaged walls, piles of rubble, dead men.

"Now listen to me carefully," Travis said. He pulled a piece of parchment out from under his shirt and pushed it into Jobe's hands. "I want you to get through to General Lefferts."

"General Lefferts, sir?" Jobe asked.

"Give him this. That's an order, soldier," Travis said. "Can you do it?"

"Yes, sir," Jobe said.

"You're too young to die, son," the man said. "God be with you."

"Look out!" Jobe yelled, but it was too late. As he watched, a Mexican lunged forward and thrust a bayonet through Travis's back. The man's eyes bulged in pain, and he fell forward into Jobe's arms. The Mexican had fastened on Jobe, but even as he prepared

again to die, a shot rang out and the Mexican crumpled to the ground. "Colonel Travis," Jobe pleaded.

"Lefferts," Travis whispered. "Shuttlecock
Road."

"No, Colonel Travis, please no," Jobe said. But
there was no time for grief. More Mexicans were approaching. Jobe dropped the lifeless body and ran.
Across the compound he saw Davey Crockett, his
ammunition spent, swinging his rifle at the Mexicans
besieging him. The Mexicans spotted the boy as he
ran, and opened fire. Jobe ducked and scrambled as
bullets hit the ground at his feet.

He ran aimlessly through the smoke, followed by
the Mexicans screaming in Spanish and shooting,
when suddenly he found himself at the Alamo's front
gates. He looked behind him at the twenty Mexicans
coming up on him fast. They stopped, raised their
rifles, and Jobe stood still, calm, and closed his eyes.

An arm yanked him away, just as the puffs of
smoke left the muzzles of the rifles; he opened his
eyes and looked into the tanned face of a man in his
mid-forties, wearing a suit. On his breast pocket was
a small plastic sign which read *Jack Murphy,
Curator*. "Sorry, son," the man said. "It's closing
time."

Stunned, Jobe let himself be led through the
Alamo's gates. "Come back, now," the man said,
and swung them shut behind him. Jobe stood, his
back to the Alamo, looking out on San Antonio,
Texas.

It was 1985; though Jobe had no idea of the date,
he knew it wasn't 1836. Before him, a Woolworth's
flanked a shopping mall, a gas station, a branch of
the Lone Star Bank. The Alamo was dwarfed by the
city. He walked, putting one foot before the other, to
the edge of a cement sidewalk where a bus stood,

inscribed with green letters spelling CROCKETT TOUR-LINES. The man who stood by the door with a blue hard-rimmed cap said, "Get in, son. I haven't got all day."

Jobe mounted the steps, and the driver jumped up after him, swung the doors shut, and pulled out into the San Antonio traffic.

He stood in a daze as the bus pulled out, until the man said, "You'll have to take a seat." All day, Jobe had been doing as he'd been told, and he turned away and stumbled back, as the bus lurched, toward the other passengers. "Next stop on our tour of San Antonio," the driver said, "is the Civic Center, home of the San Antonio Spurs."

Jobe stopped beside a kid with a big pink bubble expanding from his mouth, and an elderly woman across the aisle, wearing a wide-brimmed straw hat. She patted the seat beside her and said, "This one's free." Automatically Jobe sat down, and the woman began talking. All Jobe could think about was the parchment in his pocket. He had to find Shuttlecock Road. He had to get the message to General Lefferts.

"I'm traveling with my grandson," the woman said, "but he's not one for sightseeing. Said he'd rather spend the day in the motel pool." Jobe wanted to be polite, but didn't know what to say. "I'm Harriet Wendsell from New Haven, Connecticut," the woman said.

"Jobe Farnum, ma'am. I have to find—"

"What an original outfit!" the woman said. Jobe looked down at his soiled buckskin; most of the fringe had been torn. On his head he wore a coonskin cap. "Where are *you* from, Jobe?"

"The great free state of Texas," Jobe said. He began to look around him in amazement at the people on the bus.

"You Texans are worse than New Yorkers," the woman said. "The great this, the great that. Do you go to school here, Jobe?"

"No ma'am," Jobe said. "I'm a volunteer, and I've got to find—"

"A volunteer!" the woman said. "How wonderful. You know in this day and age it's hard to find anyone willing to volunteer for anything. Everyone wants to know what's in it for themselves."

"Please, ma'am," Jobe said. "I've got to get to Shuttlecock Road."

"Is that the opera house?" the woman asked.

"No, ma'am," Jobe said. "General Lefferts is there."

"I don't think there's a General Lefferts on this tour," the woman said.

"Please, ma'am," Jobe said. He could hear his voice beginning to rise in pitch; he was afraid he might faint.

"Driver!" the woman called. "This nice young man wants to get to Shuttlecock Road."

The driver called back, "I'll have to let him off downtown; he'll have to transfer to the Q14 bus."

"There, Jobe," the woman said, settling back. "That's taken care of."

The driver stopped, he walked off, and the bus left in a cloud of blue exhaust. All around him tall buildings rose into the clouds, or so it seemed to Jobe; traffic swirled, horns honked, people hurried by. Jobe was pushed out of the way as he stood, disoriented, on the sidewalk. Though he tried to stop the people, to ask where Shuttlecock Road was, no one listened; they all ignored him, tried to keep from touching him.

Finally Jobe saw a six-year-old boy who pointed something at him, and he had a moment of panic.

But then he saw it was only a toy. "What's that?" he asked.

"A laser gun," the boy said proudly. "Got you. I bet you're hot in that." He pointed to Jobe's outfit.

"Yes," Jobe said. "I am."

"Want some?" The boy extended the paper cup he held in his other hand.

"Thanks," Jobe said. The liquid in the cup was dark and full of bubbles; he took a small sip. "What is this?" he asked.

"Root beer," the boy said.

"Do you know where Shuttlecock Road is?" Jobe asked.

"I'm not allowed to cross the street," the boy said. "Do you live there?"

"No," Jobe said. "General John Lefferts is there, and I've got to find him."

The boy pointed to the corner, where a man stood with his shoulder against a rectangular box made of something like glass. "Look in the telephone book," the boy said. "That's what my mother does." He took Jobe by the hand and walked with him to the corner. The man in the phone booth hung up and stalked away. The boy showed Jobe the book. "Do you have any money?" he asked.

Just then a frantic woman in short pants and a very skimpy top rushed up to the boy. "Sam!" she said. "I'm going to have to put a chain on you if you keep running away. You scared me to death."

"He doesn't have any money, mommy," Sam said.

The woman glanced at Jobe with obvious distaste. Jobe couldn't keep his eyes off the woman; she looked practically naked to him. "All right," the woman said, handing Jobe a round coin. "But I will not give money to every poor stranger you meet." She began pulling Sam down the sidewalk, away from Jobe.

Jobe turned, picked up the receiver as he'd seen the man do, and held it to his ear. "General Lefferts," he yelled. "Shuttlecock Road." But nothing happened. After standing there for a minute, he looked at the receiver, let it drop, and hurried down the street.

Not far from the phone booth, he found a group of boys about his age, with black skin, spinning around on their backs while the sounds of someone shouting came out of a gray box. The tallest of the group came up to him and said, "Yo, bro. I dig your funky cap. I'm Master Blaster Jack and I'm the Universal King of Rap." He stuck out his hand and gave Jobe an elaborate handshake Jobe had a hard time following. "I'm a lean mean rap machine, you know what I mean. And you got the threads that's turning my head." He grabbed Jobe's coonskin cap and darted across the street.

Jobe yelled in surprise and took off after him, right in front of a car with a blue and red bubble on top. The man driving it screeched to a halt and jumped from the car. "Hold it right there, buddy," the man said. He was dressed completely in blue. "You're jaywalking. I'm going to have to cite you."

"Where is Shuttlecock Road?" Jobe asked.

"Half a mile due east," the man said, and began writing on something in his hand.

"Thanks," Jobe said. He walked out into the street. All of a sudden a large red truck bore down on Jobe, the driver leaning on his horn. Without thinking, Jobe raised his rifle and put a bullet in the truck's radiator. The truck skidded to a halt, steam rising from the engine.

"Hey, you!" the man who'd been writing yelled. Jobe looked back. The man was on one knee, sighting down the length of his arm to his hand, which held a pistol. Jobe took off.

• • •

Things got complicated after that. Running from the blue man, Jobe darted in and out among the crowds of people. He turned a corner and came upon another man dressed entirely in blue, standing next to a horse while he talked to a woman. Jobe dashed up and in a running mount took off on the horse as the sound of sirens filled the air.

The police chased him down a one-way street which ended in a cul-de-sac, past old tattered men sipping from green bottles and sitting with their backs against the wall. As the sirens and cars came closer, Jobe bore down, and with his urging, the horse made a breathtaking leap, up and over the wall at the end, leaving the police behind. On the other side were more cars and more stores and more people, and the approaching sounds of even more sirens.

Jobe wheeled and rode the horse into an underground parking garage. He pulled the horse up next to a truck and quieted its fear; he didn't have to wait long before more police with bubbles on their cruisers and flashlights in their hands began walking among the parked cars and trucks. Jobe's heart was in his throat, but he kept quiet, and the horse was soothed by the darkness, and after a little while the police shrugged, went back to their cars, and sped out of the garage.

He rode the horse up into daylight again, turned left, and there at the end of the street was a patch of green, a park with trees and playing fields. Jobe headed directly for it, rode through softball games and young men playing Frisbee, through a family picnic, across a basketball court, scattering the players.

He cantered through the park; on the other side, he found what he'd been looking for. The road sign said

Shuttlecock Road. But which way should he turn? He turned left, and rode the horse up onto a grassy mall.

Suddenly he was in the middle of it again. People carrying shopping bags reeled back in fear; the horse was terrified, and so was Jobe.

The horse reared; Jobe finally pulled it under control and sat astride it, yelling, "General Lefferts! Please. Someone lead me to General Lefferts." He climbed off the horse and held the reins in his hands, searching the faces of the crowd which had gathered. Finally one man walked forward.

"Please," Jobe said. "I need your help."

"What's the matter, son?" the man asked.

"Please," Jobe said. "The Mexican army! Thousands of them."

"Are you lost?" the man asked.

"I've got to find him. Don't you understand?" Jobe said. "There's no time. Santa Ana's men, they're overrunning the Alamo."

"Take it easy, boy. Calm down," another man said.

"Don't you see?" Jobe said. "If we don't defeat Santa Ana, there won't *be* a Texas any more."

"I know, son. I know," the first man said.

"I gotta find General Lefferts," Jobe yelled. "Come on! If you love Texas, you'll pick up a gun and ride with me!" He pulled a pistol from his belt and held it high.

The people backed away at the sight of the gun. A woman dropped a bag of groceries and in the stillness Jobe heard the sound of shattered glass.

"Give me the gun, boy," the first man said, stepping forward. Jobe saw the second man trying to grab the horse's reins.

"You're all crazy," Jobe yelled. He leapt back on the horse and took off at a gallop down the mall.

It wasn't more than another block before he saw the sign: LEFFERTS' ANTIQUES. He pulled the whinnying horse to a stop, dismounted. It was dark and gloomy inside, full of old knives and guns and other paraphernalia, and for the first time since he'd left the Alamo, Jobe felt at home.

A man came through a door at the back of the shop, a man in his early thirties. "Can I help you?" he asked.

"I'm looking for General Lefferts, sir," Jobe said.

"Who?" the man asked.

"General John Lefferts," Jobe said.

"I'm John Lefferts," the man said, "but . . . "

Jobe pulled the parchment Travis had given him out of his shirt and thrust it at the man. "This is for you, sir," he said.

Lefferts carefully unfolded the parchment and studied it, looked up at Jobe, then back to the parchment. His face was a mixture of bewilderment, suspicion, and shock. Jobe found a knife in a glass-covered case marked NOT FOR SALE and said, "That's one of Jim Bowie's."

"Yes," the man said. "It was." He held out the parchment and shook it at Jobe. "The gunpowder burns are still fresh. And the blood . . . Where did you get this?"

"Colonel Travis, sir," Jobe said.

"Colonel Travis?" The man turned back to the parchment. In the case with the Bowie knife was a silver belt buckle with the initials JHF on it, his initials. He turned his own belt buckle up and looked at it; the two were identical.

Jobe tapped the glass case and said, "This is from the Alamo."

"Yes," the man said. With an eyepiece, he was now studying the parchment Jobe had given him.

"What happened there?" Jobe asked.

"Where?"

"At the Alamo."

"Everybody died," the man said. "Every last soul." He removed the eyepiece and looked at Jobe. "I don't know how you got this," he said, "but it's authentic. How much do you want for it?"

"Sir?" Jobe asked.

"How much money do you want for this?" the man asked.

"I don't want any money for it, sir," Jobe said.

"Look," the man said, losing patience. "This is real. It's a message from Colonel William Barrett Travis to my great-grandfather on the day the Alamo fell."

In the distance Jobe heard the high whine of sirens. "I have to go now," he said.

"Wait a second!" the man said.

"I have to get back," Jobe said. "I did what I came to do. I have to get back to help."

"Back where?" the man asked.

But Jobe didn't answer him. Outside, he jumped on the horse, and took off down the mall. He rode until he came to a gas station, where a boy about his age was polishing the windshield of a car. "Excuse me," Jobe said. "Which way to the Alamo?"

The boy looked at him, shading his eyes. Jobe could see he couldn't quite believe what he saw. "That-a-way," the boy said, pointing.

"Thank you," Jobe Farnum said. He wheeled the horse, took off in the right direction, back to join the others. From what he'd seen today, the pushing and the shoving, the whining and the yelling, the avarice and selfishness, he would be happy to achieve an honorable death.

THE SECRET CINEMA
by Steven Bauer

Based on the Universal Television series *Amazing Stories*
Created by Steven Spielberg
Adapted from the episode ''The Secret Cinema''
Teleplay by Paul Bartel

POOR JANE! FOR SEVERAL WEEKS, HER LIFE HAD been falling apart at a rate even more furious than the rate of dissolution which had caused her to see Dr. Shreck in the first place. Now as she lay on his couch in his darkened office, she found herself trying to keep from telling him the most recent catastrophe. Dr. Shreck seemed to find Jane's troubles amusing; far from offering her explanations for her feelings, or sympathizing in some way, he took great pleasure in uncovering what was happening to her and directing her in a course of action which, so far, had been disastrous.

Poor, poor Jane! But what did she know about analysis, after all? Maybe this was part of the treatment, maybe she had to get worse before she got better, maybe it was all that *trans* word. Transport?

Transferral? It was so confusing.

"Now, Jane," Dr. Shreck was saying. "You mean nothing at all happened this week that you want to talk about?"

She opened her eyes and peeked at him; he sat behind his massive walnut desk and in the gloom he seemed to be smirking at her, and leaning forward to get a better look.

"Nothing that I can think of, doctor. I cleaned my apartment. I went shopping for new towels . . . " She knew she'd have to tell him. Why was she so hesitant? It was that *other* word, resistance.

"Jane," Dr. Shreck said, the coaxing parent.

"Oh yes, of course," Jane said. "How silly of me to forget. Yesterday I broke off my engagement to Dick."

"Would you like to discuss it?" the doctor asked.

Jane closed her eyes, decided to make the best of it. "Dick is very immature, doctor. Not ready for marriage," she said. "I hated to hurt his feelings, but I had to think of myself first." Her lip started to quiver as she remembered what had really happened. "He'll just have to get along without . . . " Her voice simply stopped working.

"He dumped you, didn't he, Jane?" Dr. Shreck asked.

Tears welled in Jane's eyes. "Oh, Dr. Shreck," she said. "I still don't understand what happened. It was the strangest evening of my entire life." Now the details appeared before her eyes almost as though she were watching a movie, and she told her analyst all.

She'd entered the front door of Dick's apartment, wearing a white veil, a silly surprise, but then both she and Dick were pretty silly. "Here comes the bride!" she sang, cheerful and jaunty, to the strains of "The Wedding March." She struck a pose, like a mannequin in a store window, and accidentally knocked a vase off the small table by the door. Or did she? Anyway, it fell to the floor and shattered.

"Jane!" Dick said. "Try to control yourself. What's that thing on your head?"

He sat across the room in his favorite chair, dressed in khaki slacks and a long-sleeved white shirt, tieless, holding a sheaf of papers in his lap. He didn't stand up to greet her; he just sat there.

"Do you like it?" she asked. "It's my bridal veil. I know it's bad luck for you to see it before the wedding but . . . "

"I think you better sit down," Dick said. "I have something to tell you."

Cautiously she crossed to the chair he motioned her toward, and sat down primly, her knees together, her hands pressed in her lap. "Don't tell me you couldn't get a reservation at the Honeymoon Hotel," she said.

"Jane, dearest," Dick said. "The wedding is off."

She stared at him blankly, trying to understand. Then the chair collapsed. All four legs slid out from under her and she found herself sprawled on the floor, tangled in white netting and chair legs and cushioned upholstery.

"Jane," Dick said coldly. "That was an original Chippendale. You owe me seven hundred dollars."

"What do you mean?" she said, struggling to her feet. "We've just invited two hundred people."

Dick glanced at the papers in his lap. Then, very quietly, almost whispering, he said, "I want you to turn around and lick your lips."

"My lips?"

"Then turn slowly back to me and ask if there's another woman." She stared at him. "Do it!" he said.

Obediently, she turned around, licked her lips,

then turned back and said, "Dick, is there another woman?"

"Of course not," Dick said, indignant and flushed. "Silly little fool. Whatever gave you that idea?" Then, *sotto voce*, he said, "Move a little to your left." Without thinking, she did as she was told. "That's better," he said.

"Dick," she said bravely. "Last night you said you loved me. You *said* you wanted to live with me forever."

"You've got the emphasis wrong," he hissed. "For*ever*. Emphasize for*ever*."

"What?" Jane said, now thoroughly confused.

"Like this," Dick said. He turned away, licked his lips, and when he spoke to her again, his voice was a quavery falsetto. " 'Dick,' " he said. " 'Last night you said you loved me. You said you wanted to live with me *forever*.' Got it?"

"What's going on here?" she said. "Do you feel all right?" She felt an impulse to rush to his side, to feel his forehead, to bring him water and chicken soup.

"Well," he said. "If you must know, I'm dying."

"Dying!" she said. "That's ridiculous. You just had a physical. The doctor reported you were in perfect . . ."

"Well, not dying, exactly," Dick said. "It's like dying. I'm moving away. To Sweden. For the winter sports."

This took her completely by surprise. "I'd like to get out of the city, too," she said. "But why Sweden? What's wrong with . . . Vermont?"

"Oh brother," Dick said. "I need a drink. Would you hand me that glass on the table?"

Though the glass was empty, she moved toward it resolutely. "Dick," she said. "Whatever the problem is, I know we can work it out. It would be such a shame to let our destructive impulses ruin . . . " She heard Dr. Shreck's voice saying those words, getting her to rehearse them as she lay on the couch. She picked up the glass and the table flew apart. Its top cracked in two and fell to the floor in neat pieces. Its four legs slanted outward from the center. A bowl of fruit crashed in shards and an orange rolled over her foot. In alarm and dismay she dropped the glass.

"My table," Dick said. "Jane, honestly."

"I'm sorry," she said, though truly she didn't know what for. "I don't know how that hap— Dick, you're making me so nervous." Her hands were trembling; she felt weak in the knees.

"Never mind," Dick said. "It was just an old antique."

"I'm terribly sorry," she said. "I'll pay to have it fixed."

"Just get me some soda from the icebox, will you? And try not to break anything else."

Gingerly, she stepped from among the table's ruins, trying not to ground the shattered crystal into the floor; she gave the broken chair a wide berth. "Dick," she said, crossing to the icebox. "Why don't you relax and let me make dinner?"

"Be careful when you open the door, Jane," he said. "It's very, very full."

Exasperated, she looked at him and said, "I'm not a *complete* klutz, you know."

She pulled the refrigerator handle and the door came off and crashed to the floor beside her, almost wrenching her arm off. But she had no time to worry about that. From the refrigerator's interior came a landslide of food, crates of lettuce and oranges, cases of milk and cartons of juice, six or seven dozen eggs, jars of pickles and jam and olives as well as several roasts, cascading to the floor around her.

Then the custard pie flew out of the fridge and hit

her in the face. She stood, astonished, as the gooey custard began sliding off her cheeks in sheets.

"That was our *dinner*, Jane," Dick had said, standing at last. "The pie was going to be our dessert."

That was all of it; she hadn't held back a single shameful, humiliating detail. In analysis, of course, she knew complete honesty was an essential. She was sobbing into a Kleenex. "And that's the whole story," she said. "I feel like a complete failure, Dr. Shreck."

"Jane, Jane," the doctor said. "These feelings of confusion and inadequacy you have experienced are easily explained." Why did he seem to be laughing?

"Is it my infantile Oedipus complex?" she asked.

"No, no, no," Dr. Shreck said. "Jane, the underlying fundamentals of your basic problem seem to be rooted in your clothes."

"My clothes?" Jane said, opening her eyes wide and staring at the doctor. She was wearing a very basic, very utilitarian gray wool skirt and matching jacket over a cream-colored blouse, the model of the modern working woman. "My clothes?" she said.

"And your makeup and your hair," the doctor said.

"But Dr. Shreck," Jane said. "Don't my problems come from deep inside me?"

"Don't you wish!" Dr. Shreck said. "Psychological problems are easy to fix. But it's very difficult to do anything about the way we look. Nevertheless, under my guidance, and with the help of Nurse, you *will* be cured."

"Doctor," Jane asked, almost breathless. "Where did you say you studied medicine?"

Dr. Shreck harrumphed, and continued. "The treatment will commence tonight," he said. "Didn't you tell me your boyfriend goes to the Movie Star Lounge every evening?''

"Yes," Jane said, "but I wouldn't dare . . . "

"Nonsense! When he sees the way you look after Nurse is through with you, his eyes will pop out." Shreck pressed a buzzer on his desk and yelled "Nurse!" into the intercom.

Immediately Nurse entered, a tall, broad-shouldered woman wearing a white uniform and white cap. On a surgical tray she carried an assortment of makeup which she placed on the doctor's desk; she drew herself into an attitude of attention.

"Look at this face, Nurse," the doctor said, motioning toward Jane. "Look at these clothes. Is there hope?"

"It's never too late, doctor," the nurse said. "A little lipstick, the right shoes, given a few weeks . . . "

"Tonight!" the doctor said, rising triumphantly from behind his desk. Was the session over? She'd only been there twenty-five minutes according to her watch. "I want her made over tonight," Shreck continued. "She has a rendezvous with destiny at ten o'clock."

"All right, honey," Nurse said to Jane. "I'll come around your place about seven, say? You got any fuchsia lipstick?" Jane shook her head. "Never mind," Nurse said. "I'll bring some."

"Doctor," Jane said, sitting up. "With all due respect, I'm not sure this is a good idea. I never wear makeup. It makes me look—"

"I'm afraid your hour is up, Jane," the doctor said. "Now I want you to march yourself across the street to the newsstand and pick up a copy of *Modern Glamour*. Study the models. Try to act and think like them. Nurse will help you. When I see you again, I expect you to be well on your way to sanity." He rang a bell on his blotter, the kind desk clerks use to summon bellboys. "Next!" he said as Nurse ushered Jane out of his office.

As she waited for the light to change before attempting to cross Fifth Avenue, her thoughts sped like the Manhattan traffic. The past six months were all such a blur, finding both Dick and Dr. Shreck within a week, and everything that had happened since. In fact, she'd tried to make an appointment with another psychoanalyst, but his line had been disconnected and a computerized voice had suggested she try another number, which had turned out to be Dr. Shreck. The week after that she'd fallen into the pond and Dick had saved her, and their romance had been a whirlwind after that. He'd proposed to her, in spite of her having gotten locked in the attic with the bats and house sparrows, in spite of the car accident, in spite of the time her panties had mysteriously filled with air and her dress had ballooned out over her hips and stomach.

But now he'd called off the wedding. The light changed and the careening autos ground to a halt, and Jane hurried across the avenue to get *Modern Glamour*. Another customer was talking to the blind newsdealer and Jane could overhear just the tail end of the conversation. "Did I laugh!" the woman said. "And when she wrecked his icebox!" She was tightly holding the hand of a small boy.

"Sounded funny to me," the blind man said.

"I wish you could have seen it," the woman said. "It was hysterical. But sad too."

Jane wished she'd seen whatever it was the woman was talking about. "Do you have a copy of *Modern Glamour* magazine?" she said timidly.

"Hey," the boy said. "Aren't you Jane?"

"You *are* her," the newsdealer said. "I'd know your voice anywhere."

"Well, I'll be," the woman said. "It's Jane."

Jane was totally amazed. "I think so," she said, "but how did you . . . "

"We've been fans of yours since the first episode," the woman said.

"Can I have your autograph?" the little boy asked, suddenly shy.

"Listen," Jane said. "I think you're both confusing me with someone else."

"Please," the boy said. "It's for my sister. She's very sick." Jane didn't want to disappoint a sick child, or her insistent brother either. She obliged. "Gee, thanks," the kid said. "I bet this is worth a lot of money."

The blind man tapped the stacks of magazines with his cane. "Some day," he said, "I bet your face will be on every one of these magazines. That'll be two dollars."

"Thank you," Jane said, clutching the copy of *Modern Glamour* and walking away.

It was Thursday, and she was late for her weekly luncheon with her mother. She hurried into the restaurant and looked around apprehensively; finally she saw her mother sitting alone, and quickly joined her.

"Honestly," her mother said, before Jane had even had time to unfold her napkin. "Once a week we have lunch together. Is it too much to ask that you be on time once a week? You may be a star to the public, but I'm still your mother. I've already ordered."

"I'm sorry, mother," Jane said. "I've just had the most terrible week. Dick called off our wedding, and . . . "

Her mother waved her hand. "Please," she said. "Don't tell me any more. I don't want you to spoil it for me."

"Spoil it for you? Mother, what are you . . . "

The waiter appeared at her side, a tall broad-shouldered man who, if it hadn't been for his thin dark mustache, would have looked very much like a woman. "Take your order, miss?" he asked. "The turkey is very nice today."

"I'll have a green salad, please," Jane said.

"Dark meat or white meat?" the waiter said.

"No, no," Jane said. "I don't want turkey. Just a green salad and a glass of iced tea."

"*No turkey?*" the waiter exploded, and then composed himself. "How about some turkey soup? It's delicious."

"How about bringing me my salad and iced tea?" Jane said.

"Well," the waiter said, drawing himself up imperiously. "You don't have to get huffy." Jane watched him stalk away; from the back he looked just like . . .

"Mother," Jane said. "The weirdest thing just happened to me. I was at a newsstand and a little boy —a complete stranger—asked me for my autograph."

"I wasn't going to say anything, dear," her mother said, "but since you've brought it up . . . " She reached into her voluminous handbag and pulled out a sheaf of eight-by-ten glossies of Jane and a fountain pen. A bright orange scrap of paper the size of a ticket stub fell on the tablecloth. "A lot of the girls in my bridge club have been pestering me for an autographed picture of you. It would mean a lot to them. Jane, are you listening to me?"

But Jane wasn't paying attention. Across the crowded restaurant, so far away she couldn't be sure, the waiter was talking to three men, two of whom looked an awful lot like Dick and Dr. Shreck. The third man was fat and loutish, and smoked a cigar. In fact, she thought he'd been lounging in a stretch limo right by the newsstand where she'd bought *Modern*

Glamour. "I'm sorry, mother," she said. "I think I'm having an hallucination."

Her mother laughed. "That's just how I feel when I sit in the theater," she said, "people all around me laughing their heads off, and I think, 'That wonderful girl up there on the screen is my daughter, my little Jane.' Confidentially, dear, how much are they paying you?"

"Mother," Jane said. "I'm afraid I'm not feeling very . . . " She picked up the scrap of orange paper; she was reading the bold black letters which said SE-CRET CINE when the waiter appeared and set down a huge platter before her, which held an entire turkey. "Here you are, miss," he said.

"But I didn't order turkey," Jane protested. "I ordered a green—"

"You did so," the waiter said. "You ordered turkey." He turned to Jane's mother. "She ordered turkey, didn't she? Nice hot turkey."

"I remember something about turkey," Jane's mother said evasively. "Didn't I go there on my honeymoon?"

"See!" the waiter said triumphantly. The restaurant had grown very quiet. Everyone seemed to be watching Jane's table.

"Well, I didn't order turkey," Jane said, "and I'm not going to eat turkey."

"Look out, Jane," her mother said nervously. "Don't cross him."

"I see," the waiter said, deadly calm. "In that case, perhaps you'd like your dessert." Some of the people in the restaurant were standing in order to get a better view.

"They have wonderful chocolate mousse, Jane," her mother said.

"No mousse for you," the waiter said. "We have only one dessert today."

"Don't tell me," Jane said. "It's . . . " Directly

above her, Jane heard a whistling noise and looked up in time to see an entire custard pie, custard down, falling into her face.

Nurse arrived at Jane's apartment at seven, as planned, and began working on her. The whole time the woman sprayed and teased Jane's hair, Jane kept trying to imagine what she'd look like in a waiter's uniform, with a thin dark mustache. "It's awfully nice of you to do this for me," Jane said finally.

"Aw, that's all right," Nurse said. "It's part of our training. Seven years at Beauty School before they even let us near a scalpel. Now, do you know what you're going to say when you see Dick?"

"I hadn't really thought," Jane said.

Nurse pulled a piece of paper out of her pocket and consulted it. "You're going to say, 'Why, Dick! I never expected to see you here. What a pleasant surprise.' Then he says something, then you say, 'Dick! Isn't this a perfect night for romance?' Go on, say it." Jane did as she was told, fumbling the lines, and Nurse said, "Close enough. Now hurry up, you're going to be late. Time is money, you know."

"Nurse," Jane said hesitantly. "Have you ever heard of something called the Secret Cinema?"

A car horn sounded outside, and all of a sudden Nurse was struggling with her coat. "Whoops," she said. "There's my taxi. Gotta run. Remember, the Movie Star Lounge, ten o'clock sharp."

"Thanks again for everything, Nurse," Jane said as Nurse slammed the door behind her. "You're a real pal," she said to the empty room. She stood and looked in the mirror for the first time. Her hair had been sprayed orange and sprang from her head as though electrified. Her lips were fuchsia, her eyelids green. Bright red rounds of rouge stood out on her cheeks. She was wearing a dress such as Dorothy wore in *The Wizard of Oz* and her legs were covered to the knees by white socks with horizontal green stripes.

The thunderstorm started about 9:45 and Jane splashed through puddles, holding her umbrella above her, as she hurried toward the Movie Star Lounge. The doorman was speaking into a walkie-talkie, and turned away from her as she passed him. She flung open the door and walked in.

Orange and blue spots strafed the ceiling, and the dancing couples who confronted her parted like the Red Sea in *The Ten Commandments* as she made her way toward the center of the dance floor where she found . . .

Poor, poor, poor Jane! Seated against satin pillows on a large double bed, naked to the waist, passionately embracing a large blonde woman, a tall, broad-shouldered woman wearing a frilly negligee, was Dick. "Oh, hello, Jane!" he said brightly.

Confused and upset, Jane said, "Why, Dick! What a surprise! I didn't expect to see you here . . . "

"Then what are you doing here?" Dick asked.

"Well," Jane stammered. "I . . . isn't this romantic?"

"Where did you get that dress?" Dick said. "You look like Dorothy in *The Wizard* . . . "

"My doctor made me wear it," Jane said, suddenly angry.

"Jane," Dick said. "I want you to meet my new fiancée. Hildegaarde, this is Jane."

The blonde turned around. She had fake black eyelashes and heavy makeup; she wasn't wearing a mustache, nor a white hat, but still . . .

"How do you do, Jane?" the blonde said.

"Hildegaarde?" Jane said. "What kind of a name is that?"

"I'm Sveedish, you know," the blonde said.

"Hildegaarde is a famous model, Jane. She and I are going to be married soon," Dick said.

"Where do you model, Hildegaarde?" Jane asked. "At a massage parlor? Dick, would you . . . "

"Have you ever tasted Sveedish meatballs, Jane?" the blonde asked. "They're delicious."

"Dick," Jane insisted. "Can I talk to you privately for a moment?"

"I think you'd better leave now, Jane," Dick said. "Hildegaarde and I are on our honeymoon. Naturally we want to be alone." As she watched, the double bed spun away from her and Dick and the blonde began kissing. Around her, rock music surged, and she began bouncing off dancers as though they were bumpers in a pinball machine.

She ran from the nightclub, hysterical, and splashed down the street. She didn't know where she'd go, or what she'd do. It didn't matter any more. She turned down an alley, the kind where muggers hide, when she saw someone who looked very much like Dr. Shreck dart into another alley leading off the first.

"Dr. Shreck!" Jane yelled, and began running. She made the corner, but the doctor was nowhere to be seen. Instead, she found herself in a cul-de-sac, surrounded by bare brick walls, facing what looked like industrial garage doors. Frustrated, she turned to leave and just then she saw a white porcelain button and a small brass plate, with a notice printed underneath it: DO NOT PUSH.

Jane felt a little like Alice about to descend the rabbit hole as she pushed it.

Behind her there was a fanfare of music; the garage doors swung open and colored lights flashed. Jane spun around. Like a pop-up book being opened, a theater marquee pushed out from within; the ticket booth with a ticket seller rose from the ground, and display windows unfolded from the side. On the marquee, in large red movie letters, were the words

THE ADVENTURES OF JANE
EPISODE 15
"BREAKING UP IS FUN TO DO"

"Excuse me," Jane said to the suspiciously familiar ticket seller, a tall broad-shouldered woman wearing a red Dynel wig and rhinestone-studded glasses. "Can you tell me who's in *The Adventures of Jane*? Is this the Secret Cinema?"

"I'm sorry, miss," the woman said. "No one may be admitted until the start of the next show."

"But I just saw my doctor go in here," Jane said. "It had to have been him. I must speak with him."

"I'm sorry, Jane," the woman said. "No one may be admitted until the start of the next show. You may wait in the lobby if you wish."

"Thank you," Jane said. The lobby was divided down the center by a glass-topped partition, on each side of which were doors leading into and out of the auditorium. From the darkened recesses of the theater Jane heard Dick's voice, amplified by a sophisticated speaker system. "Just get me some soda from the icebox, will you? And try not to break anything else."

"Dick," she heard her own voice say, "why don't you relax and let me make dinner?"

"Be careful when you open the door, Jane," Dick's voice said. "It's very, very full."

"I'm not a *complete* klutz, you know." Then she heard the sound of something hitting the floor, of things falling and colliding, and the audience responded with gales of laughter, huge applause. Before she could compose herself, the doors on the other side of the partition flew open and out streamed the audience. Among them, Jane saw her mother, her mother's bridge club, the blind newsdealer, the woman with her little boy, and other faces, from the restaurant and Movie Star Lounge.

She beat on the glass with her fist, but no one paid the least attention to her. Then she saw someone in an old-fashioned usher's uniform replacing a poster in one of the glass-covered poster boxes. COMING SOON! the poster said.

THE ADVENTURES OF JANE
EPISODE 16
"OFF TO THE ASYLUM!"

The glass before her blurred; she was suddenly very dizzy. She collapsed in a heap on the thin red movie lobby carpet.

When she awoke, she was lying beneath the DO NOT PUSH button. Somewhere a bird was chirping. She clumsily got to her feet and pushed the button. As they had the night before, the garage doors rumbled open, only this time the Secret Cinema didn't appear. What confronted Jane was a bakery, rows and rows of custard pies cooling on metal racks. Standing in the middle, holding a pie, was a baker in a white toque who bellowed, "Who pushed that button? Oh, it's you. What are you looking for, some nice fresh pie?"

WHAT JANE DIDN'T SEE

Mr. Krupp, the movie's producer, sat behind the "doctor's" desk, ruminantly chewing his cigar, while the "doctor" and "nurse" stood before him apprehensively. "It's taking too long to finish," he said, "and it's way over budget."

"Wait till you see the next episode," Shreck said. "We're going to send her to Paris without money or clothes. Then she gets kidnapped by Arabs . . ."

"Forget it," Krupp said. "I'm not putting another penny into this turkey."

"Turkey!" the nurse said indignantly. "It's a big underground hit. Everyone loves it! David Ansen said . . ."

"Yeah," Krupp said. "Well, I want it wound up in a hurry. I want a big dramatic finish. I want to see some blood up there on the screen."

"Mr. Krupp," the nurse said. "*The Adventures of Jane* is supposed to be a comedy."

"I want laughter," Krupp said. "I want tears. I want the fury of a woman scorned, unleashed against the rat who jilted her. I want it cheap. And I want it tomorrow."

When Krupp left, they called Dick. "Well, what about the blood?" he asked. "All I've got in the house is ink. You know how I hate improvisation. I like it all written down and rehearsed." Then the doctor's office bell rang. All three of them knew who *that* was.

BACK TO JANE, NOT A MOMENT TOO LATE

"Doctor," Jane said. "I'm afraid I'm losing my mind." Then she told him everything, every sordid detail, every paranoid fantasy, every hallucination, every ugly, unworthy thought.

"A conspiracy?" Shreck said. "To film your life? With hidden cameras?"

"Am I crazy?" Jane asked. "Or are they trying to drive me insane for their movie?"

"Jane," Shreck said. "This delusion is clearly a

manifestation of your trauma at being rejected by your lover. What you need is a dramatic confrontation. Go to Dick's apartment. Explain clearly how you feel. Demand that he give up this other woman. And when he refuses, take this gun and shoot him right through the heart."

He gave her the Luger from his desk drawer, and she took it.

Poor, poor, poor, poor Jane! She banged on the door, flushed with anger, ready at last to assert herself. She was tired of doing what everyone told her to do. Dick opened the door quickly, as though he'd been expecting her. "Why, Jane!" he said. "I never expected to see you here. What a pleasant surprise! Isn't this a perfect night for . . ."

"It's afternoon, you idiot," she said. "How can you smile at me and say that, after the way you've treated me? Throwing me over for another woman. You low-down, no good, son-of-a . . . of-a-ba-boon."

"Listen, Jane," Dick said calmly. "I have a favor to ask you. Hildegaarde and I are leaving for Stockholm this afternoon. Could you loan me two thousand dollars?"

"You good-for-nothing gigolo. You have the nerve to ask me for money on top of everything else?"

"Jane," Dick said. "You're not still angry about last night, are you? Come on, let's make love. I'd like to have something to remember you by."

Jane pulled the Luger from the raincoat she still wore. "I'll give you something to remember me by," she said. She pointed the gun and fired, hitting him in the chest. He stumbled backwards, a bright blue stain spreading across his shirt, and fell into his favorite chair. From nowhere, loud dramatic music, tense and discordant, flooded the apartment.

"What's that music?" Jane asked.

"You crazy little fool," Dick said. "You'll go to the chair for this."

Suddenly, Jane realized what she'd done. She flung the revolver to the floor and rushed to Dick. "Dick, forgive me," she cried. "You're the only man I'll ever love."

"It was always you, Jane," Dick said, struggling now for breath. "Fate brought us together."

"Oh, Dick," Jane cried. "Don't leave me."

"I'll love you to the day I die," he said, and died.

Behind her, Jane heard a loud banging on the door. "Open up in the name of the law!" someone shouted from the corridor. The door was kicked open and two policemen entered, one with a thin pointy beard, the other tall, broad-shouldered . . .

"Are you Jane Fitzpatrick?" the bearded one asked.

The other one said, "You're under arrest for the murder of your boyfriend, Dick. It's my duty to inform you that anything you say may be held against you in a court of law."

"I didn't mean to do it," Jane said. "He left me for another woman."

"That's all very well, little lady," the two policemen said, together. "But Crime Does Not Pay!"

The music came to a thunderous climax, and stopped abruptly. "All right," the bearded cop said. "That's a wrap. Strike the set."

Immediately, Dick's apartment was flooded with light. An army of grips and technicians appeared and began pushing back walls, disconnecting lights, carrying off furniture. Dick jumped up and walked over to Jane. The two policemen took off their uniforms.

"What is this?" Jane said. "What's going on?"

"Didn't you hear?" Nurse said. "It's a wrap."

"Wait a minute," Jane said. "Then I'm not crazy after all? There really was a film being made of my life?"

"We finished five days early and just a little over budget. If Krupp wasn't so cheap, we'd have champagne," Shreck said.

"But what about my therapy?" Jane asked.

"I hereby pronounce you completely cured," the doctor said.

"What about you, Dick?" Jane asked. "I guess you're not really marrying Hildegaarde."

"There is no Hildegaarde, Jane," he said. "And I'm Bill Stone. It's been great working with you the last six months." He clapped her on the shoulder and walked off.

"Jane," Shreck said. "Would you mind signing this release? It's for TV syndication."

"Just a second," Jane said. "If I'm the star of this, shouldn't I have a contract? Shouldn't I be getting paid? Don't movie stars make lots of money? I better talk to a lawyer."

"I cured you, didn't I?" Shreck said. "What more do you want? All right, don't sign the release. Talk to your lawyer, see if I care. Just remember one thing: Without me, you're nothing. If you walk out that door, you'll never work in this town again."

Jane, to her eternal credit, walked out that door.

But that isn't the last we'll see of Jane. In fact, she isn't poor Jane at all any more; she's very, very rich. Look, for example, at this headline from *Variety*: "JANE" WOWS WORLD.

And look at Dr. Shreck and his nurse as they run from their creditors, after having waited for their check from Mr. Krupp, who assured them it was in the mail; watch as they walk down the street, as Shreck fails to see the banana peel on the sidewalk.

Nurse helps him up, and says, "Honestly, people are such slobs. Imagine, leaving a banana peel right in the middle of the sidewalk." She picks it up; meanwhile, the doctor opens the door to his convertible and climbs in. "Well," he says, as Nurse walks to the driver's side and opens the door. "If worse comes to worst, we can always sell this car. It's supposed to be a classic. Don't slam the door."

As Nurse slams the door, the entire car collapses, the hood and trunk springing open, the doors falling off, leaving doctor and Nurse sitting in the shell of an automobile as the garbage truck parked in front of them goes into reverse and begins to approach.

Listen as the driver of the garbage truck leans out and yells, "Excuse me, doctor. I'm missing a banana peel. You didn't happen to see it anywhere, did you?" The driver looks surprisingly like the blind newsdealer you may remember.

"Don't say anything," Nurse hisses. "Pretend this isn't happening."

But the man spots the banana peel Nurse holds and says, "Oh, there it is. Just toss it in the back of my truck, will ya? I'll open it for you."

He pulls the lever and the back of the truck yawns open and buries doctor and Nurse to the neck in a deluge of garbage. A crowd begins to form, in time to marvel as Jane herself pulls up in the biggest, whitest open touring car in the world, driven by a handsome young chauffeur. Remember her orange hair and Dorothy dress? Now she's elegantly coiffed and she drips with fur boas and diamonds. Beside her sits Krupp, smiling broadly, lighting a cigar with a twenty dollar bill.

"Doctor! Nurse!" Jane trills. "What a surprise! Isn't this a perfect night for romance? Guess what? Mr. Krupp and I are getting married. I'm starring in his new film, and I owe it all to you. Here's a little token of my appreciation.''

Laugh as Jane produces a pair of perfectly matched cream pies and pitches them in doctor's and Nurse's faces. Thrill to the sound of laughter and applause as you, too, put your hands together and clap as the camera pulls back, including us all, all of us acting out the stories of our lives. And don't forget to tune in next week: Next week, it's *your* turn.

GATHER YE ACORNS
by Steven Bauer

Based on the Universal Television series *Amazing Stories*
Created by Steven Spielberg
Adapted from the episode ''Gather Ye Acorns''
Teleplay by Stu Krieger
Story by Steven Spielberg

WHEN YOU'RE MY AGE, OF COURSE, IT'S HARD TO remember exactly what you were like as a child, but I have a pretty good idea. I loved comic books and baseball, and lying out on a summer's night with my hands behind my head, watching the stars blink on and off. I loved lemonade, cocoa, my mother's beef stew. I liked pennies and Lionel trains; I liked listening to the radio. I wasn't what you'd call very ambitious—whenever I thought about what I wanted to be when I grew up, I imagined being a highwire aerialist or a rodeo cowboy or a prospector.

But that was just fine, because my parents had ambitions enough for me to last a lifetime. They knew, from the minute they discovered I was a boy, that I would be a doctor. Jonathan Quick, M.D. I'd make house calls and reassure anxious parents; I'd save the life of some U.S. congressman and become his personal physician.

Doctor, doctor, doctor, that's all they ever talked about. And of course an only son doesn't want to disappoint his parents.

The house I grew up in was comfortable but a bit shabby. My father worked at the lumber mill; he'd started there as a boy and had scrambled up the ladder a little each year until he'd become a foreman. He wore a white shirt to work, even though when he came home it was more gray than white from the dust and grit of the mill. Our living room had an old worn sofa with noticeable springs and my mother had crocheted antimacassars for its back. My father's chair was a big lumbering thing with stuffed arms broad enough to put a dinner plate on. My mother's credenza needed a new coat of varnish, but it was always freshly dusted as were the photographs of her parents and my father's parents, a few pictures from their wedding day, and others of me as a little boy. But I was never much of a one for furniture; I liked the rug and the bare ground.

The day my life turned around was a Friday in late August of 1932. I lay on my stomach reading a *New Fun* comic book, listening to "Dutch Masters Minstrels" on the old Motorola. From the kitchen came the mingled odors of onions and beef being browned; it was the weekend, and as always we were having stew.

My mother came bustling in, wiping her hands on her apron, full of the smells of her kitchen. I looked up at her as she nudged my behind with the toe of her slipper.

"Get up from there, will you please?" she said. "Your father's due any minute for lunch and he'll have himself a conniption fit if he finds you in front of the radio again."

I tried to hear the "Minstrels"; the show was almost over. "Listen to me, Jonathan," she said. "Why can't you be reading that medical book he bought for you? He could have gotten a new coat with that money and I don't believe you've opened that book once." She stalked over and clicked the radio off.

"I'll miss the best part," I yelled, sitting up quickly.

"Too bad," my mother said. "You were supposed to sweep the front walk. And what about that mess in your room? You are the laziest child in ten counties, I swear it." She was blocking the Motorola. Just then the smell of something burning came from the kitchen. She grabbed the textbook my father had bought—it was for college, and there I was, only twelve—and dropped it on my foot. "Go on now," she said, as if shooing a dog. "Go outside and do some reading." She shook her head as she hurried back toward the kitchen. "Dreaming and reading the funnies is no way to make a success of yourself."

The trouble was, I didn't much care; I'd rather have been fishing.

But she was my mother, and my father could make a big noise when he got angry, so I lugged that old book outside and sat down under the elm in the front yard. I opened it and stared at some of the pictures, but the only one which interested me was the chart of the reproductive system. Still, if you've seen those charts and drawings, you know they leave a lot to the imagination. So I closed the book and sat back, imagining. Then the acorn dropped in my lap.

I looked up and saw the squirrel; he was busy as could be, running along the elm's branches with his ratty tail—I could hear the *scritch* of his claws on the bark. He had an acorn in his mouth, and I watched as he put it in a small hole in the trunk and then went back for another. All God's creatures but me, it seemed, were worried about the future.

I went back to dreaming, which is what I did best. An acorn hit me on the back of the head; then another one hit me.

I jumped up, furious at the squirrel, but he was nowhere to be seen. In his place was a creature I could barely see, so well was it camouflaged. It was about three feet tall with a beard of gnarled tree roots and a thick thatch of green leaves where a person's hair and eyebrows should be. Its face was quite red, and its mouth was open, laughing.

At first I thought I'd really fallen asleep, but I rubbed my eyes, and when I opened them again he was still there, peering down at me.

"What are *you*?" I asked, though I knew the question wasn't polite, one my father would have disapproved of profoundly.

"Mother Nature's only son," he said, "and I would like a word with you, Jonathan Quick."

"How do you know my name?" I said. "Is this a dream?"

"Don't insult me, boy," the creature said. "I'm as real as you are, more or less." He reached to a lower branch and swung down closer to me, until he was sitting, waving his legs right above my head. He pointed to the textbook which had fallen to the ground.

"You despise that, don't you?" he said. "You'd just as soon pitch it in the lake." I nodded; though I'd never told my parents, the idea of being a doctor had never appealed to me. "Then do it!" the troll said. "And tell them once and for all that doctoring isn't for you."

"But it'll break their hearts if I don't go to medical school. It's all they've ever talked about."

"So what about your heart?" the troll asked.

"Isn't *it* worth listening to?"

"I just wish they'd give me time to be a kid," I said.

"An aspiration I heartily applaud. Be a child as long as you possibly can." He jumped down from the tree and began pacing before me, his leaves rustling in the hot summer wind. His voice became gruff, annoyed, as he stopped and pointed a finger at me. "If hard work," he said, "is such an almighty virtue, then why do so many folks drop dead from it? And try to argue with this, gossoon: All earning money does is make you want more of it."

Getting that off his chest seemed to calm him down a bit. He began pacing again, but he was no longer agitated. "There're too many doctors in this world already, and not many good ones. Seems what we really need is a few more dreamers."

"But you can't make a living out of dreams, you know," I said.

"Your father's voice," he said, and he was right. "And are you so all-fire sure? I've seen the future, gossoon, and it's quite ridiculous. Listen to me: Hang on to those things most precious to you, and I promise you'll be richer than any doctor, lawyer, or businessman you'll ever know."

"Sounds swell," I said. "Want to tell me how?"

"Stop bumping your gums," he said. "Let's see. You'll need a car; any old junk heap will do, but be sure it suits your style. And if you ever clean out your room, never throw away those things you love, no matter how much your mother carries on; there's treasure galore up there."

"Honest?" I said, because that's what *I'd* always believed.

"Yes, sir," the troll said. "And beyond that: Listen to nature; watch the squirrels—it's not by accident or luck that they survive. Lag behind long enough, gossoon, and the world will catch up to you." He turned toward me, wiggled his leafy eyebrows, and whispered, "I'm Mother Nature's only son and I speak the simple truth." Then he was gone. I mean, gone. Poof! He disappeared.

When something like that happens, one tends to pay attention. I did my best in high school without straining; I spent a good amount of time fishing during the summer and playing baseball and touch football during the spring and fall. When I was a junior, my father got me a job as a laborer at the mill so I could save money for medical school, so I went to work and saved and saved.

The night before the big day, July 17, 1938, I got home from work at the mill all hot and sweaty and in a hurry. I'd been full-time since I'd graduated. My mother sat in the rocker with her bifocals on, darning; my father sat in his chair, as always, reading the paper. They were good honest people, tired from living arduous lives, and they looked barely alive as they sat there, keeping up with the ways of the world —the holes in socks, the weekly business report.

"There's dinner for you in the oven, Jon," my mother said. "It won't take a minute to warm it."

"No time," I said. "I'm late already. I'm closing up Mr. Bieler's drugstore for him tonight; did you know his daughter's getting hitched? Sandy Bieler?"

"But you worked all day at the mill," my mother said. "Aren't you exhausted?"

"I'm all right," I said. "And besides, Mr. Bieler is paying me extra on account of it's such short notice."

My father looked up from his paper. "So it's *that* kind of wedding," he said.

"Elmer!" my mother said, looking from him to me, shocked. As far as she knew, I still believed in storks; I winked at my father, and then I said what I'd come home to say.

"I've got a surprise. For both of you," I said. "In fact, how about if I take us all out to lunch tomorrow. My treat."

"We'd love it," my mother said, without even consulting my father. I gave her a big kiss on the forehead, then went into the kitchen to get a glass of milk. I could hear them talking, though they tried to keep their voices hushed.

"I wish I knew what's bitten that boy. Ever since he finished school, he's been working nearly nonstop," my father said.

"I expect," my mother said proudly, "he must almost have his medical school tuition saved by now."

"It does this old man proud to see how he's turned out."

"He's quite a boy," my mother agreed. "Now if I could just get him to clean up that room of his."

Before I detail my parents' disappointment, let me tell you what bothered my mother about my room. First, it was always dusty because I didn't let her in with her soap and water; second, it was cluttered. I was always a bit of a packrat, could never bear to part with anything which had once been important to me. Though I was no longer twelve, I still had my Lionel train car with Mickey Mouse on one side and Minnie on the other; I had every comic book I'd ever bought, stacks and stacks of them. My clothes were always scattered in a line from the door to the bed, where I'd discarded them when undressing for sleep. And there were my treasures, an Austrian mug my grandmother had given me in which I kept handfuls of pennies, my framed and autographed photo of Lefty Grove, the American League's Most Valuable Player from 1931, an eight-inch metal Hubley revolving monkey cage toy, the clarinet I'd played from third to seventh grade.

These were the things I'd grown up with, the things I took with me when I left home the following autumn. But I'm getting a little ahead of myself.

July 18 was a beautiful cloudless day; the temperature was in the low 70s, and a warm sweet breeze was blowing. Although I wasn't with them, I know almost exactly what my parents must have said to one another as they waited for me to arrive to take them to lunch. I'd slipped out early before either of them was awake, leaving a note on the kitchen table to expect me around noon.

Even now, when they're both long dead, I can see them standing, waiting, right outside the house, my mother in her party dress with blue cross-stitch on the cuffs and hem, my father in his starched white shirt, wearing a too-wide tie. My father complained about having to dress up on Saturday, and my mother chided him; after all, it never killed anyone to put on a clean shirt, and their son was taking them out for lunch and the least they could do was look halfway decent. My father must have mused about what the surprise was, and my mother told him she knew I'd been accepted at college and had chosen this time to tell them about it.

Now it was the middle of summer, and they'd never seen me fill out a single application; but dreams for your children die hard, and they stood there expectantly when I drove around the corner in my 1933 LaRue Streamline. It was bright red, with chrome grids and bumpers, and the longest, ugliest fins you've ever seen. It had a horn that went *ahooga* and I'd spent just about every penny of the money I'd earned on it. I felt like a king must feel sitting on his throne; I felt richer than all the Rockefellers put together. I was completely in love.

But I could tell from the expression on my parents' faces, as I'd warned my friend with leafy hair and eyebrows, that I'd broken their hearts.

That fall I spent dreamily washing and waxing the LaRue, and my father stopped speaking to me. I can see him stalking toward me down the driveway, perhaps after a walk around the neighborhood, perhaps getting home very late from work.

"Evening, pop," I say to him and take a good sniff of autumn air. Somewhere, someone's burning leaves, and that pleasant acrid smell is everywhere.

But he doesn't say a word, just walks right past me as though I'm not even there. He goes into the house, letting the screen door slam. I pause and look after him, sorry for him, then go back to polishing a fender.

Then the yelling starts.

"It's just a phase, Elmer," my mother says.

"It's more'n that and you know it," my father retorts.

"He's going to be fine," my mother says. "You know what a hard worker he is."

"*Was*," my father says. "That side of him is dead and buried. He worked hard long enough to buy that car, and that was the end of it."

"Let me talk to him," my mother cajoles.

"Won't do no good, Alma," my father says, his voice rising. But my mother comes outside in the gathering dark and stands hunched in her sweater, gripping her arms with her clenched fingers.

"Aren't you going to work again soon, Jon?" my mother asks, but like that time I lay on the floor in the living room, I just don't answer, keep on polishing. "Don't you care that you're killing your father?" she asks.

"He's killing himself," I say, selfish as only an

eighteen-year-old can be. "He's gotten his dreams confused with mine."

"So what's to become of you? Waxing this heap and sitting under trees watching squirrels won't put food on your table."

"I wish you wouldn't worry so much, Ma."

"Worry?" she yells. "Of course I worry. Are you crazy? How could I not worry?"

The screaming brings my father out and he rushes over to me and rips the rag from my hand. "I've had as much of this as I can take," he yells. "I've supported you and your cockamamie schemes long enough—*no more*! You cause us nothing but aggravation."

"Elmer, no," my mother says, knowing what's coming.

"Don't tell me no," my father storms. "I say yes. He was a no-good lazy child, and now he's a no-good lazy adult. Throwing away his tuition on this car, collecting crap in his room like the junkman downtown." He turns to me and delivers the *coup de grace*. "You are nothing but a bum, and I want you out of my house."

It didn't take long to pack. I took my clothes, my mug, my toys and comics, my photo of Lefty, my clarinet and monkey cage, and a picture of the two of them taken on their wedding day before I was born and brought them worry and aggravation. I took my chamois cloths and cans of motor oil and car wax. I drove away without looking back. In the rearview mirror I saw them framed in silhouette against the soft lights of the living room. And I could have sworn, as I drove past the elm, I saw the troll, his hair and brows now the muted reds and golds of autumn, looking down on me and smiling.

I wandered here and there, to the East Coast and

the West. I worked for Barnum & Bailey as a roustabout; I was a grease monkey in New Orleans, a beach bum in Malibu. I tried my hand at prospecting in Colorado, just working enough to stay alive, but no harder. I found I liked the desert—the smell of sun burning the sand and dirt to a mirage, the jaunty look of cactus, the surprising flowers that bloom in the spring after a rain. But I was getting tired of being so poor, looking so wretched, feeling so down. My hair was matted and dirty, my clothes were tattered, my skin dried and burned by the sun. I was out of money. The troll's advice had been a load of bad luck; my parents had been right.

I'd been to the nearest town in the LaRue and returned to find a brand-new Jeep parked outside my tarpaper desert shack, two children, a boy and a girl, at play in the back. It was 1955 and I was thirty-five.

I pulled the LaRue alongside the Jeep and got out; both kids looked like jackrabbits, ready to bolt. "Hi," I said. "I won't hurt you. Who are you?"

The boy, who was younger, didn't answer, but the girl said "Elizabeth" in a timid little voice.

"What a marvelous name!" I said. "I was in love once with a circus lady named Elizabeth." The kids looked at each other and giggled. "But she was in love with the strong man. And what a strong man he was. One day he lifted Margo the Elephant right up in the air to free a clown she'd accidentally sat upon. Can you imagine? Lifted an elephant right up in the air."

A man came around from behind my shack wearing a short-sleeved white shirt and a rep tie, carrying a clipboard. "Hey," the man said. "What are you doing with my kids?"

"He was telling us a story," Elizabeth said.

"A circus story," the boy said.

"Yes, well, never mind," the man said. And then

to me: "This your place?"

I nodded and he stuck out his hand. "Paul Tread-well," he said. "Boon Development Corporation. I've got bad news for you. This land's been sold. A big resort is going up here before long."

"Where am I supposed to go?" I asked. I'd been there about six months, and had thought of settling in.

"Seeing as you were squatting in the first place, I don't think that's my concern." He smiled, got into the Jeep, and drove away. Elizabeth tried to wave, and he pulled her roughly into her seat.

I was in sad shape; if I'd had a bottle of something, I would have drunk it down. I had tears in my eyes, and it was hard breathing, such a weight of despair lay on my chest. Instead, as I'd done so often before, I began putting my stuff in the battered steamer trunk I'd picked up along the way.

Where he came from I don't know but I knew who it was the minute I heard his words. "Hi-ho, gos-soon," he said.

I whipped around, furious, with a chipped teapot in my hand. "*You!*" I yelled. He stood there plac-idly, his hair and eyebrows now covered with tumble-weed.

"Whatever happened to that sweet-faced dreamer I once knew?" he said.

I threw the teapot at him but he ducked; it ex-ploded against the flimsy wall, showering the room with fragments.

"You're what happened to me," I yelled. "You ruined my life." I grabbed two cups and threw them both, one after the other. The troll picked up a metal Coke tray and used it as a shield. "I'd like to throttle your stubby little neck," I said.

"Oh, you're a beaut, you are," the troll said, sticking his head from behind the shield. "I made no promises I didn't keep."

I looked around for something else to throw; sorry to say, I didn't own very much else. "*This* is the wonderful life you told me about?"

"You didn't want to work," he said, "and you haven't."

All I could find was a sack of flour; in midair it burst open into a shower of dust. "You said I'd be rich," I yelled.

"So I did," the troll said. "But *rich* is a relative term."

"But I have nothing—my parents are dead, thanks to you, no family, no friends . . . " I threw (what a sacrifice!) the rest of my small bag of coffee beans, and missed with that as well.

"You still have your treasures," the troll said mildly.

"They're not treasures," I said. "They're nothing but a bunch of junk, worthless memories of a wasted childhood."

"That's your father talking, gossoon."

He was right again. "I know," I said, exhausted and bitter. "It's just a damn shame it took me so long to listen."

Of course they built Las Vegas on the desert where I'd lived, and the irony wasn't lost on me. Thirty years later, 1985, and I was sixty-five years old and running out of gas on my way across the Mohave, running once again from southern California, running right toward Vegas, where I used to live.

I still had the LaRue, the one thing I'd taken care of over the years, polishing it when I could, repairing it if anything went wrong and I had the money to fix it. But this was a 1933 automobile, mind you, and zipping past me from Los Angeles, in their Lincolns and Datsun XKEs and Jags and BMWs were the wealthy people, going to hear Wayne Newton at the Sands, going to drop five thou on roulette.

Time had not been good to me. I looked, I'm ashamed to say, like a mass murderer. My hair hung lank and gray to my shoulders; I hadn't shaved in years. Had I been naked to the waist, every one of my ribs would have stuck out, like the bleached carcass of something the coyotes, sun, and wind had picked clean. Dirt had worked itself so deeply into my pores, I looked as though I'd been tattooed all over.

I was creeping into Vegas on Interstate 15, heading east, when the gas gauge finally told its sad story. People leaned on their horns as I pushed the LaRue to the shoulder and began the long haul to a gas station; but I wasn't about to strand the LaRue out there on the highway, so I grunted and shoved, nudging toward a leaded pump.

I was out of breath and near collapse when I finally pushed my car into an all-night station, and I stood, sweat streaming from me, soaking my clothes, taking great gulps of the dry desert air. A cocky gum-chewing teenager in a white uniform, his hair all cut and brushed in a punk style, swaggered up to me and stood with his hands on his hips as if he didn't speak English.

"Fill her up, please," I said. The kid took a hand off a hip long enough to jerk it at the "Self Serve" sign; then when I went to do it myself, he held the nozzle and pointed to another sign: PLEASE PAY IN ADVANCE.

I stuck my hand in my pocket and pulled out a button, some sand, and lint.

"Get outta here, you tramp," the kid snarled.

I remembered the pennies. "No, wait," I said and hobbled to the back of the LaRue, let the trunk fly up and rummaged through until I found my old mug chock full of pennies. When I brought it to him, the kid was smoking a cigarette.

"Here," I said. "There must be at least ten dollars in there. I'm gonna buy one last tank and take a fast ride over the edge of Hoover Dam.''

"There are faster and cheaper ways to take care of that," the kid said. "Don't waste your money. Besides, don't you think I've got anything better to do than count your flippin' pennies? Come back with some real money; maybe then I'll sell you gas." He left me there holding the mug as he locked the pump and went back inside, where I'm sure it was air-conditioned, slamming the door behind him.

I thought about what the kid had said and thought of all the other ways; but as I imagined dying a hundred painful deaths, and all far away from my LaRue, a stretch limousine pulled up, the back window whirred electrically down, and a white-haired woman leaned out. "Excuse me, sir," she said. "I'm sorry to bother you, but I couldn't help noticing that mug of yours. Is it a Toby?"

"I don't really know, ma'am," I said, though I thought I remembered some talk about that years ago. "All I know is that it was a present from my grandmother, and I've been keeping these same pennies in it since I was five years old."

"Do you mind if I have a look at it?" she asked.

I walked over to her and handed it in through the window. "Careful, now," I said. "All the pennies make it heavy."

Well, she looked and she looked at that old thing, turning it this way and that, looking at the green marks on the bottom, and then she said in a very level voice, "I can hardly believe it. I've collected these all my life and I don't believe I've ever seen one like it. It's magnificent. Would you consider parting with it?"

Now, it did have sentimental value, but I was in a tough spot. "How much?" I asked, used to folks taking advantage of me.

"I'm prepared to give you twenty right here on the spot," the woman said without hesitation.

Twenty dollars would feed me one last time and get me to the Hoover Dam in style. "If it would bring you pleasure," I said, "then why not?"

She was thrilled. "You wait right here," she said. "I'll have my driver take me to Vegas and we'll return with a cashier's check for twenty thousand dollars."

She misinterpreted the look on my face, and she reached out and grabbed the tatters of my jacket. "I hope you don't feel cheated," she said. I shook my head. "It's a treasure," she said. "A wonderful treasure indeed."

I started looking through the trunk more carefully after I was washed, shaved, well-trimmed, and sporting new clothes. I tried a store that specialized in comic books, and the two brothers who owned the place, David and Jerry Milgram, said things like . . .

"Holy cow!" Dave said. "A 1939 *Marvel Mystery* Number One. I know a guy in New York who just got thirty-five grand for this, and it wasn't even *nearly* in this kind of shape."

"Oh no!" Jerry said. "Do you know what this is? It's the *Action Comics* that has the very first Superman in it."

"Worth twenty grand easy," Dave said. "Collectors go out of their minds for this stuff." Then he saw the toys; he pulled out the Lionel train car with Mickey and Minnie. "Hey, Jerry," he said. "Check this out."

"Wow," Jerry said. "I'll bet old man Cundey would pay three or four grand for this, easy." Then *he* saw the monkey cage and pulled it out.

"Is that a Hubley?" Dave asked. "Shoot, I want that for myself. Then he turned to me. "I'll tell you what, Mr. Quick. Comics and toys for two hundred thousand. Flat fee for the package, right here, right now. You in?"

• • •

The rest of the story is pretty easy to figure out, I guess. I came upon an antique road rally in progress, everyone dressed in thirties clothes and driving thirties cars, and people clustered around the LaRue like a pound full of hungry dogs greets anyone who visits. Seems there weren't many LaRues around any more, and while everyone agreed it was as funny-looking now as it had been in 1933, they all said it was worth, oh, a quarter of a million dollars.

But the biggest surprise was my photograph of Lefty Grove. I'm sitting at Sotheby's in New York, dressed to the nines, and fitting in with all these beautifully tailored and styled men and women, and the auctioneer gavels the crowd to silence and says, "Our next item is this 1931 photograph of Lefty Grove, the American League's Most Valuable Player in that fine year, a photograph made remarkable not by the subject so much as by the photographer. This is a Butch Nation original platinum print. We'll start the bidding at ten thousand."

I sat there, calm as could be, as the bidding went higher and higher—fifteen, eighteen, twenty—finally turning around to see who was so anxious for the Strand. I saw, instead, two rows behind me on the aisle, an empty seat right next to my friend the troll. He seemed to be enjoying himself immensely, though he wasn't bidding. His hair and beard were snow-swept and blustery; it *was* February in New York City.

I excused myself and slipped into the empty seat beside him and whispered, "I think perhaps at the very least I owe you an apology and a drink."

But even as I spoke, the troll disappeared, and in his place was a very attractive woman, about forty-five or fifty, with fine high cheekbones and auburn hair piled on her head.

She looked at me, a bit startled, and her cheeks

colored. "I don't believe you owe me an apology *or* a drink," she said, and turned back to the auctioneer. The Strand was now at thirty-three.

I looked at her again. Her eyes were the color of my favorite cat's-eye marbles as a kid, green-yellow and cracked, and there was something playful about the way her lips twitched as she stared at the auctioneer which made me think she didn't really belong at Sotheby's. Nor did I. "But I wouldn't mind a drink," she said. My instincts weren't totally dead.

"Well," I said. "How about some dark jazzy place in the Village? Or how about the Lone Star Cafe? You look like a displaced Texan."

She laughed at that, and someone in front of us *shuush*ed us. "Bourbon and branchwater," she whispered back. The Strand topped at forty-two, and I knew I'd be sorry to see it go, but I wasn't sorry to leave before the next item was auctioned off. I was thirsty and ready to talk to Francine Guzzetta, my companion for the afternoon, who didn't mind having a bourbon and branchwater with a distinguished-looking elderly gentleman with an unusual past.

Reader, I married her.

DOROTHY AND BEN
by Steven Bauer

Based on the Universal Television series *Amazing Stories*
Created by Steven Spielberg
Adapted from the episode "Dorothy and Ben"
Teleplay by Michael de Guzman
Story by Steven Spielberg

THE NIGHTMARE BEGAN THE DAY MY DAUGHTER fell off her bike. Mind you, from what we heard later from Mrs. Pomeroy who saw the whole thing happen, the accident was nothing unusual. Dorothy was riding along our residential street in Naperville, Illinois, her back straight, her blonde hair whipping behind her, when the front wheel hit a pothole and the handlebars wrenched themselves free of her hands; the bike stopped short, and she was thrown. Parents are used to accidents like that; gauze pads, Merthiolate, and a good cry usually begin the healing process.

Only Dorothy hit her head as she fell, hit it hard. And Mrs. Pomeroy's wavering voice called out her name a few times before she realized our daughter wasn't getting up.

When my wife got to where she lay, Dorothy was breathing shallowly; the scalp wound, though ugly, didn't look life-threatening. But she didn't wake up, not then, not at the emergency room. After she'd been moved to St. Luke's in Chicago, Dr. Templeton, who specializes in comatose patients and their care, was the one who told us the news—he didn't know when Dorothy would wake up, and she might never.

We began our vigil at St. Luke's. We got the best private room, I took an indefinite leave of absence from the office—I had a lot of time coming; the company owed me. And we sat by her bedside, saying her name over and over like a charm, an incantation. We stroked her forehead where a large bruise discolored her perfect skin. She looked as if she'd been playing a game of Civil War Soldier, the crown of her head encased in bandages. If it hadn't been for the respirator, the monitoring instruments, the tubes in her nose—all the paraphernalia of modern science—it would have been impossible to know she wasn't just sleeping.

"That's what it's like," Dr. Templeton told us. "It's just like sleeping, but a kind of sleep you and I have never had."

We sat there day after day. A week went by; another week. Our nerves had been stretched to the breaking point. We were irritable with one another and with the doctors, because nothing seemed to change. My wife Samantha was pale, with large dark circles under her eyes, as if she'd gotten into a fight at the local tavern. Her hair, blonde as Dorothy's, hung lank and uncared-for.

When the old black man entered the room, we were both shocked, and then angry.

He walked in and said, "I'm fine, Dorothy. How

are you?'' He stood there in a hospital smock, bending slightly forward as if trying to hear. His eyes were
brown as melted chocolate, and his old balding head
was wreathed in a semi-halo of white hair. Samantha
was instantly on her feet and moving toward him, her
hands up as if to push him physically from the room.
Her voice was low and flat. ''How dare you come in
here?'' she said. ''This is a private room. Get out.
Leave us alone.''

The old man's face wrinkled in bewilderment and
he took a step back. ''I'm sorry,'' he said. ''Excuse
me. It's just that I heard . . . '' He looked past
Samantha's face toward where Dorothy lay on the
bed, curled in a fetal position.

''*Get out* or I'll call security,'' Samantha said. The
old man took one last look at Dorothy and left. I felt
badly for him; I thought at worst he was a little
loony, had wandered into the wrong room by mistake. And Samantha would never have spoken to
anyone like that if she hadn't been so distraught. I
caught up with him in the corridor; he hadn't gone
far. He was standing, his head cocked in the direction
of Dorothy's room.

''I'm sorry,'' I said. ''My wife . . . I want to
apologize for her. She isn't herself since the accident.''

''She fell off her bike,'' the old man said.

''It was such a simple thing,'' I explained. ''Kids
do it all the time.''

''She's in a coma,'' he said.

''It's been two weeks,'' I said. ''I have to get back
now.'' I turned and left him standing there. It wasn't
until I'd gotten back inside that the full strangeness
of what he'd said hit me. How had he known her
name? How had he known what had happened?

Behind me, the door opened. It was him again,
looking apologetic, but driven by a force strong

enough to withstand my wife's fury. "My name's Benjamin Dumfy," he said. "With an F. Call me Ben."

"No one asked you who you are," Samantha said.

But then I realized he was responding to a question neither my wife nor I had asked. His eyes were on the bed. When they met mine, he said, "Dorothy wants her teddy bear, Max, and Arnold, her penguin. She says she wishes you'd bring Please Louise too. She misses Please Louise."

"That's her elephant," I said, as if explaining it to him.

My wife was so pale she was gray. "Listen, mister," she said. "I don't know who you are or where you come from, but you better get out of here fast. This is a sick insane joke."

He looked at her mildly, as though he had years of practice in listening to abuse from white folks. "I hear her," he said. "Can't you?"

"Nobody can hear her," Samantha said. "She's in a coma! Do you understand? She can't communicate with anyone. If she could, she'd talk to us. We're her parents and we love her."

Samantha was so upset, she hadn't comprehended what was going on. This man knew the names of all our daughter's toys. "Sweetheart, it's all right," I said. "He doesn't mean any harm."

"She has a scar on her big toe from when she stepped on a broken bottle at the beach," the old man said.

"Stop it!" Samantha yelled. She put her hands over her ears.

"It was a green bottle, rubbed smooth by the ocean."

"Sea glass," I said.

"Sea grass," Benjamin Dumfy said.

"That's what she called it," I said. "She misunderstood." I could hear my voice rising; my heart was racing wildly in my chest. If this man could really hear her, hear my daughter, then how far away could she really be? She'd seemed years away.

"I'm sorry, Dorothy," the old man said. "I can't stay too long. I'm leaving today." He turned to us and said, very formally, "I'm very sorry to have upset you. It weren't my intention. I hope Dorothy will be all right."

Slowly he turned on those thin brown legs which stuck like broom handles from under the gown. He was almost to the door when he looked back at Dorothy and said, "Me too. I've always been partial to penguins."

I got the story from Dr. Templeton. In 1947, Benjamin Dumfy took his dinghy and went out fishing by himself. The weather's mercurial on a body of water as big as Lake Michigan; a storm blew up, and before he could get his dinghy back to land, he capsized. He hit his head somehow; he had a bump the size of an ostrich egg on his forehead by the time they'd gotten him to the hospital. Anyway, the owner of a yacht heading for shore saw the accident and by the time its owner had pulled Dumfy from the chop, he was near dead. His heart stopped several times in the emergency room, but though they'd managed to pull him back, he'd never regained consciousness. He'd been in a coma, in St. Luke's, since then. Until three days before the day he walked into Dorothy's room.

A resident had been asking Templeton's opinion on an elderly woman patient when a red light behind the nurses' station had begun blinking. A machine was malfunctioning in Room 906, Ben Dumfy's room. "Where's a nurse when you need one?" Templeton had asked, and then he and Haller, the resident, had gone themselves.

They'd walked into the room, paying no attention to the man who'd been lying on his back for forty years, and studied the wall of machines. I knew the ones; they were the same ones surrounding Dorothy.

The one hooked up somehow to the brain was registering normal activity, so Templeton thought it was broken. He made a joke about getting a hammer to fix it, and then another about how the more expensive things were, the more often they broke down—he was having trouble with his twenty-thousand-dollar BMW. Neither of them was looking at the patient when his eyes fluttered open and he said, "How much money you say you pay for that car? What's it made of? Gold?"

Haller was speechless until he managed to say, over and over, "He's awake." Templeton told me he thought he was going to faint.

Dumfy said, "You don't look so good, fella. Maybe you better sit down a bit. They say you put your head between your knees, it gets the circulation circulating. You fellas don't mind if I unhook some of this stuff, do you?" he said, pulling some of the wires loose.

Templeton called Dr. Caruso, even higher in the impenetrable medical hierarchy, and Caruso was astonished and alarmed.

"Do you remember your name?" Caruso asked him.

"Benjamin Dumfy," he'd said. "With an F."

"How do you feel, Mr. Dumfy?" Caruso asked.

"Good. Great. I feel great. I'd like a glass of water."

"Get Mr. Dumfy a glass of water," Caruso told Haller. "I want an EEG and a CAT scan stat. And notify Fredericks that something . . . something unusual has happened."

• • •

They cautiously tried to explain to Dumfy about the coma and how long he'd been lying there. At first he didn't believe them—who would? —thought they were trying to pull some joke, some white man's joke on poor old Ben Dumfy who'd never done no harm to nobody.

But when he saw the liver spots on his hands, when he got a look at himself in the mirror, when he walked the halls of the hospital and saw televisions and Walkmans and when, outside one of the big tinted plate glass windows he saw the skyline of Chicago and in the foreground a helicopter landing with the victim of an auto crash—well, he had to admit to himself that some time had passed.

They had to tell him his wife had passed away, and that his son, who'd been a baby when he'd gone fishing, had grown up in time to be one of the first to die in the jungles of southeast Asia. They had to explain Vietnam to him as best they could. Where would he go? He had no family, no friends whose whereabouts were known. How do you come back from the dead and make a life?

They didn't talk about those things; they ran the tests instead. I don't know if I'll get all the names right. I've just begun speaking medicalese since Dorothy was hurt.

There was no sign of septicaemia; his liver function appeared normal—no dilated veins on his abdomen. Negative Spidernavei.

"What's the last thing you remember?" Dr. Caruso had asked.

"Hitting the water," Dumfy had said. "It was cold."

His pupils appeared normal; there was no pressure in his cranium.

"Do you remember where you were born?" Dr. Templeton had asked.

"St. Louis, Missouri," Dumfy had said.

Olfactory intact, visual acuity, optic fundi normal, pupils reacting to light equal and accommodating. Facial muscles symmetrical. Romberg test negative. Babinski negative, the sign of a subarachnoid hemorrhage.

"Did you have any dreams, Ben?" Caruso had asked.

"Yes, I did," Dumfy said.

"That's impossible," Templeton said. "There was no indication of REM."

"What was the dream?" Caruso asked.

"I was thirsty."

"What did it feel like?"

"I was uncomfortable."

"Did you drink something, in your dream?"

"Yes," Dumfy said, "but I couldn't get enough."

"What else do you remember?"

"There was these two people . . . " He stopped short and his eyes focused on a point near the door. "Shhhh," Ben Dumfy whispered, cocking his head.

"What?" Caruso said. "What is it?"

"I heard something."

"What do you hear?" Templeton asked.

"I don't know. Something. Somebody," Dumfy said.

As soon as the tests were over and he was allowed to walk, he wandered the halls, searching for the voice he'd heard, and found it in Dorothy's room.

First we had to believe, and then we had to convince the doctors. We told them about Max and Please Louise, about Arnold the penguin. I explained about *sea grass*, about the scar on Dorothy's toe that this old man could never have known about. The doctors consented to let Ben sit in Dorothy's room with us, and to watch him "talk" to her. Templeton, in particular, was skeptical.

Ben sat attentively, staring at the back of her head. Samantha held her hand, and I stroked her forearm which lay limply beside her face. Caruso and Templeton watched Ben Dumfy. Dorothy lay on her side, her eyes blank as bedsheets. Whatever she saw, only Ben knew.

"She's not in any pain," he said. "She doesn't feel anything. It's like she fell into a crack between life and death."

"Is she hungry?" Caruso asked.

"Al," Templeton said, his voice grouchy with disbelief.

"Is she?" Caruso asked.

"She's not hungry," Ben said. "She's not cold. There's no sensation of time passing."

"How do you know?" Samantha asked.

"Because I was where Dorothy is now. For a very long time."

"Keep talking to her, Ben," I asked him. "Please. Maybe you can help—help bring her back."

"I don't know," Ben said. He shook his head, and his kind, wrinkled face was worried. "I'm not a doctor."

"That's right," Templeton said, standing up. "I think this has gone on long enough. I must say . . . "

"Dr. Templeton," Samantha said. "My little girl's been in a coma for two weeks and you haven't been able to pull her out of it. Please, Ben." She let go of Dorothy's hand and reached across our daughter's still body to touch the old man. "Keep talking to her. Please."

Ben looked at Dr. Caruso, who nodded gently. Dumfy stood up and came around to take the chair Samantha had vacated for him. He sat down, took Dorothy's hand, stared into her open staring eyes. He took a deep breath, let it out slowly.

"She's sorry she rode her bike in the street," he finally said. "She was mad at you because you told her she was too young to do it herself."

My wife began to cry quietly. Of course, we'd known all along it had to have been our fault.

"But she's not mad at you any more. She's sorry. She wants to know if you"—he looked at me—"will still take her to your new office."

"Of course I will, sweetheart," I said, as if I were talking directly to her. Samantha leaned against me heavily; I knew I had to get her out of the room. She was about to break down completely and wouldn't want the doctors—or maybe Dorothy?—to see her. "I'm an engineer," I said helplessly, explaining to the walls. "She loves to play with my calculator." I found I couldn't stop myself, swept along on a wave of sorrow and regret. "Dorothy and I sit down every night and go over her homework. She's a whiz at spelling and geography, and in reading, well, she's grades ahead of herself. But at times she has problems with math. And sometimes I lose my temper. I've made her cry a couple of times. You see, working with numbers has always come easily to me. Could you . . ." I felt the tears coming, couldn't stop them. "Would you tell her I'm sorry I made her cry?"

Ben looked at us, understanding, I think, how I felt. How many things must he have wanted to say to his wife and son, both gone now, both beyond him? He turned back to Dorothy.

"They're just going out for a glass of water," he said. "Maybe for a little walk." He listened, then looked at us. "Dorothy says it's okay. But come back soon."

Samantha was sobbing now, and the tears were running unimpeded down my cheeks. "We will, baby," Samantha said. "I promise." I helped her—she helped me—out into the hall."

• • •

They brought in tape recorders, and a stenographer. Ben sat as he had all day, holding Dorothy's hand. Outside, it had begun to rain, a thunderstorm. The air was streaked with lightning, and every now and then the thunder muffled everything, making Ben's job harder. Samantha and I stood against the wall. Dorothy seemed no worse, but then she wasn't any better.

He'd been talking quietly to her all day long; where he got the strength I don't know. I couldn't have managed for more than a few minutes at a time; I kept remembering every instant we'd been short with her, hadn't had time for her. I remembered the night she'd had the "bad dream" and had come crying into our room at 4 A.M. and Samantha and I decided she was a "big girl" and shouldn't get into bed with us. "It's all right," I'd said. "Go back to sleep now." And she'd turned, utterly bereft, and slumped out into the hall, dragging Arnold behind her.

"Well, if Andy McEwen keeps tugging your ponytail, seems to me like you should ask Mrs. Springer to move him to the back of the room." Ben paused, listening. "Oh," he said. "Then you ask to move to the front of the room." Another problem we'd made little of, not wanting to call her teacher and make a fuss, not wanting to baby her.

" 'Cause they're little boys," he said. "It makes them nervous that you're so pretty. That's why they hurt your feelings. Besides, boys that age just like each other." He paused. "What's that, Dorothy? What?"

I felt the breath catch in my throat.

"*They* want you to go? Who's with you?"

Beside me, Samantha straightened, leaned forward as if trying to hear.

"A boy and a girl your age? They want you to go where?"

"What's going on?" Samantha said.

"Listen to me, Dorothy," Ben said. "Two people came for me, wanting to take me from the Nowhere Place to the Somewhere Place, but I chose to wait and see." He moved closer to her, pulled the chair up until his knees were touching the bed. "I know they're both nice, and I know the Somewhere Place looks very beautiful, but you don't belong there. You belong here with your mother and father. I *know* it looks beautiful, but it's not for you, Dorothy. It's not your time to go."

"Oh my God," Samantha said.

"This has gone far enough," Templeton said. He moved forward suddenly, as though he was going to grab Ben by the arm and wrench him away from the bed. "Everyone knows . . . " But Caruso caught him and held him, told him to shut up.

"I know it's lonely in the Nowhere Place," Ben continued. "I know you're tired, but you mustn't go with them. I'll be right here with you until you're strong enough to come home." He paused again, listening. "It's not too far, Dorothy. It's not too far to go. Take a step, come toward me. I know it's hard, but you can do it."

There was a crack of thunder loud as an explosion. I could feel my heart pounding in my temples; I was watching a tug of war, and I could see only one end of the rope.

"Yes you can, you can do it. No! Not that way, don't follow them. Come to me!" Ben said. He was very agitated now. As he strained forward, I could see the tendons in his neck, taut against the old black skin. "Dorothy, stop," he said. Then his voice got much more soothing, much more understanding. "I know they'll teach you things, but there are so many things to learn here. More reading, even more math. And you *can* ride your bike in the street. I'll teach you things, Dorothy. I promise."

Ben looked around the room; he stood and walked three quick steps and grabbed the stenographer's pencil. "Like a magic trick," he said, hurrying back. "In the mouth, out the ear; watch closely, Dorothy, I'll do it again. In the . . .

"Dorothy? Dorothy?" he said. He stood, began walking back and forth beside the bed, his hands clenched together, arguing with her. "*Please*, Dorothy. *Please* talk to me."

The room was absolutely silent; I think everyone was holding his breath. "No," Ben said. "I can't do that. I can't teach you to fly, but can they . . . can they . . . they can't *live*, Dorothy. They can't *live*. Being alive is discovering new things and learning and being able to dream and hope and feel things that give us joy like the touch of the sun on your face or snowflakes on your tongue in the winter. Or the rain, the rain on your skin, Dorothy. The cool, wet rain."

Ben went to the room's only window, opened it, and stuck his hand into the evening storm. He came back to her, touched her face, leaving tracks like tears on her cheek.

"I know you're tired, Dorothy. But you can do it. If an old man like me could do it, you can do it. You'll grow up and become a woman and fall in love and maybe someday you'll have your own little baby who you'll love like you love Please Louise and Arnold. Like your mother and father love you."

He knelt beside the bed, his hands clasped in what looked like prayer. "I know it's hard, but don't give up, Dorothy. You've got to hold on. I missed so much of my life . . . " Ben's voice cracked, and I knew he was thinking of his own family, scattered, gone. "Dorothy," he said, "please don't let go of yours."

Suddenly he was on his feet, bending over her, shouting in her ear. "No, Dorothy. *No*. Listen to me. *Listen to me*. They can't have you. I won't let them take you. Tell them . . . tell them to come talk to me.''

There was a flash of lightning, close by, and a violent rumble of thunder. Ben stood very straight; his head tilted back, and then he fell heavily, crashing against the chair and then sliding sideways onto the floor. His eyes were closed.

Templeton and Caruso rushed to where he lay. "He's not breathing," Templeton said.

"Get that chair out of the way," Caruso yelled. Caruso straightened the crumpled body until Ben lay on his back, his arms at his sides, the light brown palms peaceful, untensed. Caruso bent over, his ear near Ben's mouth; he felt Ben's neck for a pulse. His face was frightened, white; to one of the nurses he hissed, "Go, quickly! Code Blue."

The nurse ran through the door, and the whole room wheeled with motion. Caruso jutted Ben's chin toward the ceiling, opened his mouth, blew three quick breaths into him. Templeton knelt beside him, placed his hands on Ben's sternum, and began administering CPR.

The door burst open and a nurse flew in, wheeling a cart with bottles and IVs, and one of those machines they use to jolt the heart back to life. Ben's chest was bare now. Caruso inserted an IV into a slack brown arm. "Stand back," Templeton said. "All clear." He placed the paddles on Ben's chest and the jolt shook Ben's body. "Again," Templeton said. Again the body fluttered.

"I'm not getting anything," Caruso said.

I looked at Dorothy's bed. Her eyes were moving.

"I'm not getting anything," Caruso said.

"She's awake," I said. "Dorothy's awake."

"He's gone," Caruso said, but Samantha and I were kneeling at Dorothy's side, hugging and kissing her. "She's back," Samantha said. "I have my little girl again. Dorothy, can you hear me? It's mother, darling."

"I want to see Ben," Dorothy said, her voice weak and scratchy from disuse. I supported her, helped her sit up. She stared around the room, at all the people standing helplessly by, finally locating the motionless figure on the floor.

"Hi, Ben," she said. And then she cocked her head as he had done. "Much better now," she said. Her skin, her smooth young skin, was alive under my hands. "It's as pretty as I said it was, isn't it?" She paused. "But being back with my mommy and daddy's the best, you were right. What? It's getting harder to hear you."

Templeton stood as if at attention; whatever cynicism he had was gone now. Dorothy leaned forward, getting as close to Ben as she could as we held her. "I love you too," she said.

I was aware suddenly of the breathing of all the people in the room, our common human breathing we take so much for granted. I could smell the ozone from the thunderstorm drifting in through the window Ben had opened, could hear the splash of rain against the glass. I could smell my wife's sweet smell, and Dorothy's stale precious breath.

We unhooked the wires from her forehead, slipped out the IV in her arm. We helped her down from the bed so she could touch him. She kissed him gently on his wide, clear forehead.

"Bye, Ben," she said. "Have fun in Somewhere."

She turned to us, smiling, smiling as only a seven-year-old can. "He can fly now," she said.

In the dark, hushed night of the city, through the falling rain's commotion and the muffled, distant noise of traffic, I thought I heard the sound of beating wings.